'I'm not g

Matt.'

'Why not?'

'Because you don't love me.'

Matt was silent. Polly could sense the struggle he was engaged in. Was he just trying to find the right words, or had he put the shutters down so firmly on past emotions that they were impossible to locate? He *had* loved her. Polly was sure of that. The glimpses into his soul that those dark eyes had provided had made her sure, but they were buried now. If Matt could admit his vulnerability and allow Polly to step past the barriers he had erected, however briefly, there would be hope for a future together. Things wouldn't be the same, but they could be even better. If Matt was prepared to take that risk then Polly would know just how precious a gift that trust would be.

'I...' Matt hesitated and cleared his throat, and at precisely the same moment his mobile phone began to ring.

DOCTORS DOWN UNDER

In Medical Romance™ you'll find a special kind of doctor. Flying doctors, bush doctors, family doctors and city specialists from Sydney, Brisbane or Auckland. Whether they're battling with life and love decisions in the hot and harsh locations of the wilderness, or dealing with the personal and medical dramas of city life, they exude a determination, dedication and an earthy charm that only comes from Down Under.

DOCTORS DOWN UNDER

They're irresistible

From Mills & Boon® Medical Romance™

THE SURGEON'S CHILD

BY

ALISON ROBERTS

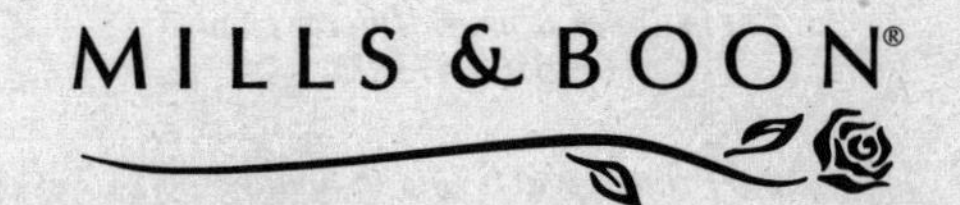

First published in Great Britain 2003
Harlequin Mills & Boon Limited,
Eton House, 18-24 Paradise Road, Richmond, Surrey TW9 1SR

ISBN 0 263 83462 X

Set in Times Roman 10½ on 12 pt.
03-0803-47362

Printed and bound in Spain
by Litografia Rosés, S.A., Barcelona

CHAPTER ONE

THE pyjamas were a dead give-away.

Their improbable, grinning tigers might just as well have been convict arrows, given that a scan of the stretch of riverside garden revealed no sign of any adult accompaniment. The wearer of the pyjamas was an escapee. It must have been a cleverly planned break for freedom, Polly Martin decided. She had only been working in the paediatric ward of Christchurch's Queen Mary Hospital for a week but she knew very well how close a guard they kept on their small charges.

As a camouflage, the tigers were a miserable failure but to the runaway's credit, they disappeared very effectively behind the screen of coprosma hedging that bordered a rose garden to the right of the path Polly was using. She veered away from the direct route towards the riverside entrance to the hospital, leaving the pathway and keeping an eye on the ground as she stepped carefully to avoid flattening the exuberant foliage of the daffodil plants that carpeted the area. By the time Polly reached the other side of the hedge and raised her gaze, there was no sign of the friendly tigers.

Polly chewed her bottom lip thoughtfully as she paused beneath the graceful trunk of an ash tree. She was due on the ward in ten minutes and wouldn't be at all popular with Charge Nurse Lee Fenton if she was late, but it really couldn't be helped. Surely it wouldn't take long to find the child and it would be irresponsible to leave a potentially unwell patient alone in the park, especially one that small. The brief glance had suggested the girl's age was no more than three or four. Whilst the August afternoon was filled with the promise of imminent spring weather, it was still not warm enough to make pyjamas adequate cover and the warmth would disappear very soon as the sun sank beneath the level of the taller trees.

Why was the child hiding? Had she been outside, enjoying the sunshine with a parent, only to wander off and become lost? No. The movement Polly had observed had been purposeful. The girl was running away and the most likely reason was that something had frightened her—maybe the prospect of an unpleasant medical procedure. Polly had to admire the courage displayed by the action. Most small children would cling to their parents. Or scream. Usually both.

'Where are you?' Polly called. She looked around as the silence swallowed her words. The manicured rose garden afforded no real cover and she was confident that the length of time her approach had taken had not been enough to allow travel to the hedging on the other side of the large garden. Polly sighed, tucking a strand of straight, blonde, shoulder-length hair behind her ear. This could take longer than she had anticipated unless she could think of something clever.

'OK. You win. You're pretty good at this game.' Polly dumped her shoulder-bag by the tree trunk. 'Now it's my turn to hide.'

The silence continued. Polly felt slightly idiotic speaking loudly to an empty rose garden but instinct told her that the child was nearby. She had to give it one more try.

'Do I have to put my pyjamas on to play?' Polly managed to sound dismayed. 'I forgot to bring them. And I haven't got any with lions on them, anyway.'

'They're *tigers*!' The firm correction came from a very unexpected direction. Polly's head tipped sharply backwards.

'Oh! You're in the tree! How did you get all the way up there?'

'I climbed. I'm good at climbing.'

'I can see that.' The bare branches of the ash tree were numerous but not particularly sturdy-looking. The child was well above head height and Polly moved a little so she could be in a position to catch the small girl if she fell.

'My name's Polly,' she said cheerfully. 'What's yours?'

'Bonnie.'

'Does anybody know you're here, Bonnie?'

'No. I ran away.'

'Oh.' Polly nodded seriously. 'I feel like running away sometimes, too. In fact, I *did* run away once.'

'Were you little, like me?'

'No. I was quite big.' Polly smiled inwardly. Twenty-seven would be far too ancient for Bonnie to relate to, and that had been a year ago now. 'How old are you, Bonnie?'

'I'm five.'

'Are you?' Polly was observing the child as best she could. She appeared to be physically very small for her age. A pale face and tiny features made dark eyes appear strikingly large. The curly hair was dark, too—what was left of it.

'Why did *you* run away?'

Polly's smile indicated that the personal question was welcome. Her heart had already been captured by an obviously spirited and probably seriously unwell child. She wanted to try and make a connection here and do something to help Bonnie.

'Something was happening that I didn't like very much,' she said honestly. An explanation of a shattered romance and broken dreams was more information than Bonnie would understand. Or need. 'So I ran away.'

'Was it going to hurt?'

The suspicion that Bonnie was escaping some painful procedure was strengthened. If she was running away then she must have prior knowledge of what was in store so it was probably an experience she had had before. Polly avoided trying to make any distinction between physical and emotional pain.

'Things that hurt aren't very nice, are they?'

'No.'

'Is that why you're running away?'

The nod came after a pause long enough to suggest that Bonnie had weighed up whether or not to trust Polly with such important information. The affirmation felt like real progress.

'Would you like to come down and tell me about it?' Polly's suggestion offered sympathy.

'No.'

'Oh…OK.' Polly took a quick glance over her shoulder. Somebody must be searching for Bonnie by now. Probably a large posse. If she waited just a little longer reinforcements would arrive and maybe someone that knew Bonnie would be able to persuade her to climb down from the tree.

Bonnie was peering thoughtfully downwards. 'You can come up here if you want.'

'I'm a bit big.'

'I can make room. See?' Pyjama-clad legs moved as Bonnie rose and wriggled further upwards. Branches swayed ominously and Polly's heart almost stopped as an anguished wail accompanied something that fell towards the ground.

'Oh, *no*! I dropped Tigger!'

Polly picked up the soft toy tiger and brushed off the dead leaves sticking to the bright orange and black fur. 'He's OK,' she assured Bonnie.

'I want Tigger.' For the first time, Bonnie sounded close to tears. Crouched on her new branch, with her arms around the main trunk of the tree, she sounded far less confident than she had a minute ago.

'Can you come down and get him?' Polly knew she sounded dubious. Bonnie was now about three metres off the ground. If she hadn't managed to catch Tigger, how would she cope with a falling child?

'No-o-o!' Bonnie sobbed. 'I'm *stuck*!'

There was still no sign of any reinforcements. Polly was on her own here.

'I want *Tigger*!' Bonnie howled.

'OK.' She had to do something. 'Just hang on, Bonnie. I'm coming.'

Polly tucked the soft toy inside her polar fleece jacket. It was easy enough to find footholds in the divisions the main trunk provided. Polly pulled herself up swiftly until she encountered a narrow gap between two of the higher branches. Squeezing through proved a challenge and Polly was panting when she paused after the effort.

'You must be good at climbing,' she told Bonnie. 'This is hard work.'

'I want to get down,' Bonnie sobbed. 'I don't like it up here any more and my legs hurt.'

'We'll get down in just a minute,' Polly said with far more confidence than she felt. If it was this hard getting up by herself, it would be impossible to reverse the process carrying a miserable child. 'Look—here's Tigger.'

Easing herself carefully upright, Polly found Bonnie close enough to touch. Holding the trunk of the tree with one hand, Polly unzipped her jacket and extracted the toy. Bonnie leaned down, only to lose her balance as she clutched for the toy. Polly grabbed hold of the small body with her free arm, hanging grimly on to the tree trunk with the other. Tiny legs wrapped themselves around her waist and a small head burrowed into her shoulder with painful determination.

'It's all right. You're safe now, pet. Everything's OK.' The reassurance was as much for herself as the child. It took several panicky seconds for Polly to regain her own balance and secure a better position before she could feel confident enough to soothe her terrified burden. She kissed the top of Bonnie's head.

'It's OK, sweetheart,' she whispered. 'I've got you. I won't let you fall.'

Loud sniffs and gurgles against her neck were punctuated by another sound. A voice close enough to hear quite clearly.

'Bonnie! *Bonnie!*'

'Over here!' Polly called.

'Bonnie?' The voice belonged to a woman. Anxiety was now mixed with confusion. 'Where are you?'

'Bonnie's here,' Polly shouted. She couldn't risk trying to turn. 'We're in the tree.'

'I've found her!' The woman sounded excited now. 'She's over here.'

'Where?' A man's voice came from somewhere behind Polly. 'I can't see her.'

'She's up the tree.'

'What?'

Bonnie stopped crying. *'Mummy!'*

'It's all right, darling. Mummy's here.'

'What on *earth* is she doing up the tree?' The man's voice was very close now.

'There's someone up there with her.' Two heads came into view and Polly found herself under intense scrutiny. Bonnie's mother was looking at her accusingly as though she were responsible for planting her daughter in the tree. Embarrassingly, the man standing beside her was Matthew Saunders, one of the consultant surgeons at the Queen Mary.

'I found Bonnie hiding in the tree,' Polly explained hurriedly. 'I couldn't leave her here by herself.'

'Of course not,' Bonnie's mother said.

'But did you have to get into the tree yourself?' Matthew Saunders was scanning the tree's structure. The pinstriped suit he was wearing did not look at all suitable for climbing, and of all the consultants Polly knew of at the Queen Mary, Matthew Saunders was probably the least likely to imagine shinnying up a tree. He was the stereotype of a highly ranked medical staff member. Conservative and aloof, he had never deigned to notice Polly's existence on the numerous occasions he had appeared in the emergency department. She couldn't remember ever having seen him smile. What was he doing here, anyway? Mr Saunders was a general surgeon but he did handle a lot of paediatric cases. Was Bonnie one of his patients?

'Tigger fell out.' Polly's level of embarrassment went up a notch. 'And then…well…'

'Is she all right?' Bonnie's mother sounded anxious again now. 'She's been missing for nearly an hour and she's not well.'

Bonnie leaned precariously to peer over Polly's shoulder. 'Hello, Mummy.'

The woman burst into tears and Bonnie's hold on Polly tightened. Her voice wobbled. 'What's wrong with Mummy?'

'She's worried about you,' Polly whispered. 'I think she needs a cuddle.'

More people joined the group at the base of the tree. Two security guards peered upwards. One reached for a hand-held radio.

'She's been found,' he reported. 'No further assistance required.'

Polly wasn't too sure about that. They might need a ladder to get down from this predicament.

'Can you get down by yourself?' Matthew Saunders seemed to catch Polly's line of thought.

'Not while I'm holding Bonnie.'

'I'll get the kid.' A burly security guard moved in and reached for a branch.

'No!' Bonnie shrieked. 'Go *away*!' She burst into noisy sobs and clung to Polly tightly enough to make breathing an effort.

'She's frightened of uniforms,' Bonnie's mother said. 'And strange men.'

'You'd better leave,' Matthew Saunders told the guards. 'We can deal with this.' He peeled off the pinstriped jacket of his suit.

Polly's eyes widened. Surely the surgeon would count as a strange man? And if Bonnie was his patient, wouldn't his approach be even more frightening for a child trying to escape medical treatment? But Bonnie seemed unperturbed as Matthew Saunders advanced up the tree. Polly watched his progress. Strong hands gripped each branch and the movements of his body made the climb seem effortless. He avoided the narrow gap Polly had squeezed herself through which was just as well. Although not particularly tall—maybe five feet nine or ten—he had broad enough shoulders to have made the gap a potential sticking point. The handgrip near Polly's foot was confident. It was hard to imagine that hand engaged in the delicate movements that the paediatric component of the general surgeon's position entailed. In fact, this whole exercise was proving somewhat of a revelation.

'Hello, Bonnie.' Matthew was very close now. 'Are you ready to come down?'

'Is Polly coming, too?'

His eyebrow was raised as he glanced at Polly. How embarrassing was this—to be only inches away from a consultant surgeon? The impression of neatness was even more pronounced close up. Fine features. Neatly groomed hair. Dark eyes and an expression that advertised reserve. Matthew Saunders was definitely the perfect picture of a consultant. Confident, skilled, very sure of himself. And very aloof.

'I've seen you around somewhere, haven't I?'

'I'm a nurse.' Polly's smile was a little tentative. 'Polly Martin.'

'Of course. Emergency department, right?'

'I started on paediatrics last week.'

'Did you? That's good.' Matthew shifted his position on the branch. He didn't expand on why he thought the move was positive. 'I'm Matt Saunders.'

Polly nodded. It was an odd place for introductions and the man was well known to anyone who had worked in Emergency. His tendency not to delegate referrals to registrars and housemen unless absolutely necessary had made the surgeon something of a legend.

'Sorry I didn't recognise you straight away.' Matthew was smiling now. 'You look a bit different…up a tree.'

'I'm sure.' Polly returned the smile with genuine warmth. It was hard not to. Matthew Saunders had a surprisingly friendly smile. She had very definitely never seen this man smile before. She would have remembered a smile like that. In fact, if she had ever seen it, she would have registered that the surgeon was rather a good-looking man. Very good-looking, even.

'To be honest,' Polly confessed, 'I'll be rather glad to get down. I think Bonnie and I have had quite enough of being up this tree.'

'Let's do something about that.' Matthew checked the security of his handgrip and reached towards Bonnie with his other arm. 'Come on, tuppence. Let go of Polly now. I'm going to carry you down the tree.'

'But I want Polly to come, too.'

'I'll be right behind you,' Polly promised. 'I can't climb down while I'm holding you and Tigger, though.'

'Uncle Matt could carry you, too,' Bonnie suggested.

Uncle Matt? No wonder Bonnie hadn't been frightened of the doctor. Surely he wouldn't be allowed to have a relative as a patient, though? Maybe he was an honorary uncle by virtue of being in a relationship with Bonnie's mother. Polly glanced down at the woman beneath them. She was an attractive woman with long, dark hair and she looked a little older than Polly. A guess of mid-thirties would be the age group that she would also put Matt Saunders in. Maybe it was a rather close relationship. The woman's body shape looked disproportionate enough to suggest she was pregnant. Or was it just the perspective of the unusual position Polly was in?

Bonnie's mother noticed the glance.

'What's taking so long, Matt? Is something wrong?'

'No. Don't worry, Karen. We'll be down in a minute.' Matthew sounded decisive. 'I'll carry you down first,' he told Bonnie. 'If Polly needs help, I'll come back up and carry her down as well.'

'OK.' Bonnie seemed satisfied with the new arrangement. She reached out with one arm and Polly found herself virtually cheek to cheek with Matthew Saunders as they transferred the child to his arms. Her earlier embarrassment had faded after they had introduced themselves but it came back now with renewed force. Polly had to extricate her hand when it somehow became wedged between Bonnie's leg and Matthew's chest. The pale blue fabric of his shirt didn't offer much of a cover. She could feel the warmth of his skin and the firm outline of his ribs. Polly closed her eyes for a second, hoping to ward off a blush, but the surgeon didn't appear to have noticed the rather intimate contact.

'Hang on tight,' he instructed Bonnie. 'I need both hands to climb with.'

Bonnie wrapped herself around him like a small monkey. Tigger's tail could be seen poking out above her shoulder. Matthew looked up as he secured a foothold on a lower branch.

'I'll come back and give you a hand, Polly.'

'I'll be fine.' Polly hurriedly began her own descent. Being carried down in Matthew Saunders's arms in that fashion was unthinkable. It was a relief to find herself standing on firm ground again.

Another man had joined the group. He had one arm around Bonnie's mother who was now holding her daughter. Matthew Saunders was brushing dead leaves off his shirt.

'I'm Russell Weaver,' the newcomer told Polly. 'Bonnie's dad. I can't tell you how grateful we are for your help.'

Karen Weaver nodded emphatically. 'We were worried sick.'

'You're very welcome,' Polly said. 'It was a pleasure to meet Bonnie.'

Bonnie raised her head from her mother's shoulder. 'I like Polly,' she announced. 'She's nice.'

'She sure is,' Russell agreed. He held out his arms. 'Let me carry you now, short stuff. Mummy's got a sore back today.'

'Have you?' Matt was putting his jacket back on. 'How bad is it, Karen?'

'I'm fine.' Karen ran a hand over her slightly rounded abdomen as Bonnie's weight was removed. 'Don't fuss, Matt. Russell has been doing more than enough of that.'

Polly tried to brush off the moss streaking her jeans

and promptly gave up. She felt uncomfortable being included in this conversation. These people obviously knew each other very well and Karen Weaver's pregnancy and any complications it might be presenting were not something the woman was likely to want to discuss in front of a stranger. Polly picked up her shoulder-bag.

'I'll have to go,' she excused herself. 'I'll come and see you later, Bonnie. I'm a bit late for work now.'

Very late. Polly was on the 3 p.m. to 11 p.m. shift. Even if she ran, it would be nearly 4 p.m. by the time she was changed and on the ward. Lee Fenton would not be impressed.

The charge nurse was worse than unimpressed. She was furious. 'What kind of time do you call this, Polly Martin? Handover's finished and Stephanie's had to stay on to cover your patients. We're flat out.'

'I'm sorry. I got caught up. There was a—'

'I'm not remotely interested in excuses,' Lee snapped. 'This simply isn't good enough, Polly, and I'm going to include it in my report.'

'I don't think that needs to happen.' Polly hadn't noticed the entrance of another person to the office but, then, Matthew Saunders moved as quietly as his appearance suggested he would. 'Polly was delayed by unavoidable circumstances. It was she that found Bonnie in the park.'

'Oh.' Lee was taken aback. 'I didn't realise. Why didn't you say something, Polly?'

Polly remained silent. It wouldn't help to point out that she had, in fact, been trying to do precisely that. The consultant's expression did not suggest any sympathy but the brief glance Polly received made her quite sure that he had overheard enough to understand the situation perfectly. It felt like she had an ally as Matt continued speaking to the charge nurse.

'I was rather hoping to have a word to you regarding Bonnie if you have a spare minute, Lee.'

'Oh...of course.' Lee looked frankly worried now. Patients in the paediatric ward were her responsibility. Bonnie's leave without absence could have had dire repercussions and she still hadn't filled in the incident report form. Her glance at Polly was dismissive.

'Stephanie will fill you in on your patients for the shift. I think you'll find her in the treatment room. Peter Stapleton is having another IV line inserted.'

Stephanie was highly relieved to see Polly. She was holding a screaming toddler as a harassed-looking paediatric registrar taped a cannula into place on the two-year-old's arm.

'Sorry I'm late, Steph. I got caught up in the search-and-rescue mission for one of our patients.'

'Bonnie Weaver? Has she been found?'

Polly nodded and then grinned. 'I was sitting up in a tree with her for a while.'

'That figures. No matter how sick she gets, she always surprises us. She's a brave kid—one of my favourites.'

'What's wrong with her?'

'Leukaemia. She's been in and out of the ward for about three years now. She was one of the first patients I ever looked after here. They still haven't achieved a total remission. I think they're considering a bone-marrow transplant this time.'

'That's awful.' Polly would have found the information sad no matter what child it was about. The instant bond she had felt with Bonnie made it a lot more distressing.

The registrar, Susie Barrett, glanced up. 'Could you find a few metres of very sticky tape, please? And an arm splint?'

'A full body splint might be a good idea.' Stephanie rocked the toddler carefully. 'Almost done, Peter. You're being a very good boy.'

She winked at Polly. Peter was far from a good boy. He had been trouble ever since he'd arrived on the ward two days ago. Toys had been broken, a fellow patient had been bitten and this was the third attempt to gain IV access that would last long enough for the course of antibiotics that Peter needed for his pneumonia.

When the cannula in Peter's arm had been secured as impenetrably as Fort Knox, Polly returned him to his room. She had another patient in the same room who needed care. Four-year-old Laura was suffering the discomfort of a herpes simplex virus that had affected her eyes. The heavy bandaging currently blinding her had probably been the reason she hadn't escaped Peter's attack yesterday. Laura's mother sighed heavily as she watched Polly deposit Peter into his cot.

'How long is it going to be before we can go home?'

'We'll bathe Laura's eyes again now up in the treatment room. I can get Susie Barrett to check them while we've got the bandages off if you like. She might be able to give you a better idea of how much longer the treatment is going to take.'

'They were much less swollen this morning when

the dressing was changed. She can almost open one eye now.'

'The swelling in the eyelids isn't the main worry, though,' Polly reminded the mother. 'It's the ulcers on the corneas. If they don't heal well, it could lead to scarring and a loss of vision.'

The dinner meal trolley was being wheeled past Polly by the time she left the treatment room again. She hurried towards the sluice room to dispose of the soiled dressings. Laura's eyes were improving but her mother was likely to have to stand guard duty for another day or two. Maybe she could be moved into one of the single rooms, then her mother could have a bed to sleep in instead of the armchair the larger rooms had available for parents. Bonnie had probably gone into one of the single rooms. Karen might well need the space and opportunity to rest as much as Bonnie did.

Polly soaped her hands carefully before rinsing them. Hopefully, when the rush of serving and feeding the evening meal was over, she could find which room Bonnie was in and spend a few minutes visiting. Aware of someone entering the room behind her, Polly turned her head, expecting to greet a colleague. Seeing Matthew Saunders in the sluice room was just as astonishing as seeing him climb a tree. He looked vaguely uncomfortable himself.

'I just wanted to thank you for your help with Bonnie this afternoon.'

'Is she OK?'

'Pretty exhausted. She's asleep now. She's been asking for you.'

'I'll pop in and visit later when she's had a rest. What room is she in?'

'Room One. Karen's staying with her.' Matthew cleared his throat. 'I had a word with Lee Fenton. I've requested that Bonnie be assigned to your care whenever you're on duty. She's taken quite a shine to you.'

'It's mutual.' Polly smiled. 'She's a delightful little girl.'

'You do know that her prognosis isn't great?' Matt was watching her carefully. 'She's been admitted for extensive tests to see whether a bone-marrow transplant is a possibility. Even if it is, the chances for a cure aren't very high.'

'I understand that.' Polly allowed her gaze to remain on the watchful dark eyes as she reached for some paper towels. 'I'm very sorry.'

An eyebrow rose fractionally and Polly crumpled the damp towels nervously. Was she taking an unwelcome step over a professional boundary?

'It's hard enough when they're patients,' she added quickly. 'It must be so much worse for you.'

'What makes you say that?' The tone was guarded.

'Because...' Polly felt slightly confused now. 'Because...you're Bonnie's uncle, aren't you?'

'No. I'm not her uncle.'

'Oh.' Polly deposited the used towels in the rubbish bin and avoided Matt's gaze. 'Sorry, I misunderstood.'

'I'm Bonnie's father.'

Polly's jaw dropped. 'But she has a father. Russell Weaver. I met him in the park.' Her voice trailed away as she caught the odd look she was receiving.

'Bonnie was adopted. I'm her birth father.'

'Oh...' Polly said again. Her mind was racing. The Weavers did all seem to know Matt rather well. Surely that wasn't usually the case, even in today's more open adoptions. Had the Weavers been chosen as adoptive parents because they were already close friends? Or had it been some sort of surrogacy arrangement? Polly's curiosity was tempered by suspicion. It seemed a rather weird set-up, whatever the reasons.

'I'm telling you this in strict confidence,' the surgeon said quietly. 'My relationship with Bonnie Weaver is not something I want to become common knowledge around the hospital.'

'No. I'm sure it isn't.' The words popped out in a tone that surprised Polly as much as it did Matt.

His eyes narrowed slightly in the pause that followed. 'Is keeping a confidence a problem for you? Or is it just the nature of the confidence that you find distasteful?'

'It's really none of my business.' Polly's voice tightened. 'I'm sure you had the best of reasons to give your child up for adoption.'

Maybe Bonnie had been the baby of a mistress he'd had. Or maybe his wife had died and he didn't have the time or commitment to try raising the child himself. Or maybe…

'Perhaps you're right.' Matt's face had closed. His tone was clipped. 'It *is* none of your business.'

He turned sharply and walked out of the sluice room. 'Let's forget we ever had this conversation, shall we?'

CHAPTER TWO

A REQUEST to forget her own name might have had a similar chance of success.

Especially when Polly was so closely involved with the subject of the revelation she was supposed to erase from her memory. Lee clearly hadn't forgotten any instructions Matthew had left her with. Instead of helping with the usual ward routine and caring for three or four assigned patients, Polly found herself specialling Bonnie from the moment she left the sluice room.

Susie Barrett arrived in Room One shortly after Polly. She eyed the IV tray placed on the locker and Polly heard a small sigh. She smiled. Polly had the feeling that this patient was going to be much less of a challenge for Susie than young Peter Stapleton had been.

'Who's going to go first, Bonnie? You or Tigger?'

Bonnie's fearful expression was banished by her surprise. A small smile curved the corners of her mouth with a distinctive upward tilt. A tilt that was very reminiscent of Matt's smile.

'Tigger.'

'OK.'

Karen visibly relaxed at her daughter's interested tone. She smiled at Polly gratefully as she positioned the soft toy tiger on Bonnie's lap.

'You hold one paw,' Polly instructed Bonnie. 'To

keep him happy. And I'll hold the other one so it stays still enough for Dr Susie to find a vein.'

'What's a vein?'

'It's a little pipe that carries your blood. When we put the special tube inside it then we can take samples and give medicines without having to use any more needles.'

'Tigger doesn't like needles.'

'I know.' Polly stroked the well-worn and obviously treasured toy. 'But I think he's going to be brave.'

Susie obligingly participated in the pretence and Polly found the distraction welcome, although it didn't entirely banish the thoughts persistently flitting through the back of her mind. Why would Matthew Saunders have told her—a complete stranger—something so personal and potentially damaging?

Polly had never heard the slightest hint of gossip about him. As far as anyone knew, he was a dedicated surgeon who kept his personal and professional lives entirely separate. People liked him well enough. He was considered highly competent in his field and his interpersonal relationships with his colleagues never included confrontation. He was a quiet man. Conservative and predictable. Boring, in fact.

Polly shook her head fractionally as Susie completed inserting the cannula into the toy tiger's leg. Boring men didn't have secrets like that. And boring men didn't go around climbing trees at the drop of a hat either. Polly taped the luer plug into place and reached for a small bandage.

'He's brave, isn't he?' Polly said with admiration. 'Do you think that's because he was allowed to sit on your knee?'

'Tigers are always brave.'

'You like tigers, don't you, Bonnie?'

'I *love* tigers,' Bonnie said decisively. 'Daddy painted trees on my bedroom wall at home and I'm allowed to stick pictures of tigers there. I've got lots and lots.'

'Sounds like a jungle.' Polly could see Bonnie looking apprehensive again now that it was her turn for the procedure. 'Would you like to sit on my knee, Bonnie? You can still hold Tigger with one arm and Mummy can hold your hand.'

'OK.'

Polly held the child close. Unlike Peter Stapleton, Bonnie didn't struggle and only the tiniest of whimpers escaped when the needle pierced her skin.

'You know something?' Polly whispered. 'I think you're just as brave as any tiger.'

Bonnie needed to be brave.

The lumbar puncture scheduled for the following day to check for leukaemia cells in her cerebrospinal fluid was a procedure anyone would have found frightening. The little girl had to be held in position, lying curled up on her left side to lengthen her spine. Surgical drapes had been placed with only the lower back exposed and the skin had been painted with bright orange disinfectant.

Karen was with her daughter again and was dressed, as were Polly and Susie, in a gown and mask. Another person entered the treatment room as Polly pulled on a pair of gloves to assist Susie.

'I'll have a gown, thanks,' Matthew Saunders ordered.

Polly handed him a gown. And a mask. She even tied the gown for the surgeon, but the look she received was not one of gratitude. The briefest of eye contact was entirely impersonal. Almost rude, in fact. Polly snapped her gloves into position and moved to the trolley beside the bed.

'What gauge needle do you want, Susie?'

'I'll have a twenty, thanks. Can you check the stylet while I draw up this local?'

'Sure.'

Polly had to concentrate on her task but she kept up a good level of cheerful encouragement for both Bonnie and Karen during the procedure. She ignored Matt. Infiltrating the area with local anaesthetic was the worst part for Bonnie. After that she had to keep very still but she was unaware of the needle entering the space in her spinal column or the tense moments of waiting to see whether the position was good enough to provide easy collection of the required sample.

Sedation was given the following day when Bonnie had a full MRI scan. Polly accompanied her patient to the radiography department but could only wait in the outer chamber while the scan took place. Both Russell and Karen were present and Polly wasn't surprised when Matt joined them halfway through the procedure. She didn't have to ignore the surgeon this time. He ignored her.

Excluded from the group, Polly sat and listened while Matt discussed his impressions of the emerging pictures.

'There seems to be more bone involvement than last time,' he concluded heavily. 'It's no wonder her pain level has been increasing.'

'Will she still need to have the bone-marrow biopsy done?'

'I'm afraid so. They're waiting for us now in the oncology department and we may as well take advantage of the level of sedation Bonnie's under. She'll be able to have a good rest this afternoon. I'll make sure you don't get disturbed by any more testing today.'

'You must be so proud of Bonnie.' Polly shifted the pillow slightly under the small head. The dose of morphine she had just administered following their return from the bone-marrow biopsy had had the desired effect and Bonnie was now soundly asleep. 'She's such an amazing little girl. I can't believe she ever managed to climb that tree with the amount of pain she has to cope with.' Polly tucked Tigger more securely into the crook of Bonnie's arm. 'She's got the kind of spirit that's a real inspiration. I'm going to think twice before I complain about anything in the future. And she still has a smile for everybody.'

'Especially you.' Karen was smiling herself. 'Bonnie adores you, Polly. It's making this admission so much easier for all of us.' She watched as Polly posted the used syringe into a sharps container.

'It's so ironic, having to give Bonnie morphine for pain relief.'

'Why is that?' Polly reached for the chart on the end of Bonnie's bed to record the dosage and effect of the narcotic she had administered.

'It was awful when she was born, watching her go through withdrawal symptoms. Bonnie's adopted,' Karen confided. 'Her birth mother was a drug addict.'

'Really?' What on earth was someone like Matthew Saunders doing, having a relationship with a drug addict? Maybe the woman had been a prostitute. Polly's opinion of the consultant surgeon took another dive. Not that it had much further to fall before it hit rock bottom.

Over the last two days, the surgeon had been treating her as though she had done something unpardonable. She hadn't forced the man to confess anything so why should she be punished for having reacted to the astonishing information in a less than positive manner? Maybe he was trying to ensure that she didn't start spreading gossip. And no wonder. There might be quite a few things that Matthew Saunders would prefer to keep quiet.

Well, he had nothing to worry about. She had no intention of talking about the man from now on. Or talking *to* him, for that matter.

Karen leaned over to kiss her daughter gently and then sank into the armchair beside the bed.

'We knew about it, of course. We were told about Bonnie and went to see her within a couple of hours of her birth. We knew it was going to be rough but we both wanted her so much. Knowing what she had to go through just made us want her more.' Karen smiled sadly at the memory. 'She was several weeks premature. They'd delivered her by Caesarean when her mother had been admitted after an overdose. She was so tiny! And she looked so vulnerable, all wired up to those machines. Russell and I practically lived in the neonatal intensive care unit for weeks. Right from the start it felt like she was our baby. I'd had six miscarriages by then. We'd given up hope of ever having children ourselves.'

Polly laid the chart down and pulled another chair closer to Karen. It was her job to care for Bonnie and that meant supporting her parents as best she could.

If Karen needed to talk then she had the time to listen, no matter what other tasks might be waiting.

'We were so happy the day we got to take her home,' Karen continued. 'We thought the worst was behind us and we could get on with being a real family. The adoption process was a breeze. The mother didn't want any part of an open adoption. Bonnie was going to be exclusively ours.'

'Open adoptions do seem to have a few pitfalls,' Polly agreed. 'Depending on how much contact the birth relatives want, I guess.'

'I used to think that, too,' Karen said. 'But finding Bonnie's birth father was the best thing that could have happened for us. He's become a part of our family over the last couple of years.'

'Does Bonnie know who he is?'

'No, but we'll tell her as soon as she's old enough to understand. She thinks he's just a special friend. She calls him Uncle Matt. Oh!' Karen bit her lip and looked horrified. 'Oops! I didn't mean to use his name.'

'It's OK,' Polly forgot her intention not to talk about Matthew Saunders. 'I know who he is.'

Karen gaped in surprise. 'How do you know that?'

'He told me himself. The day that Bonnie was admitted.'

Karen blinked. 'Why did he do that? He's always been so careful to keep it quiet. It's never even been recorded in her notes.'

'I don't know,' Polly admitted. She had to admit she was still curious herself. Maybe if she hadn't reacted in such a censorious manner she might have found out. 'Perhaps he felt I should know because I was going to be so involved with Bonnie's care. That way I wouldn't be surprised if he was visiting her frequently.'

Karen looked unconvinced. 'Matt's always kept hospital visiting to a minimum. He thought it would make things difficult for us if staff started gossiping.'

Difficult for whom? The Weavers or himself? Polly wondered uncharitably. 'Don't worry,' she assured Karen. 'It's certainly not information that's going to go any further as far as I'm concerned.'

Karen nodded. 'I'd hate anything to make it awkward for Matt. Bonnie adores him. They're very like each other—have you noticed?'

Polly returned the nod reluctantly. She had noticed. The small features and the dark eyes. While Matthew's smile was not as frequent as Bonnie's, they had the same quirky upward curve at the corners.

'I've been worried that someone's going to spot the similarities and ask questions.'

'I think you'd have to be looking for them,' Polly said. Had she been looking for them? Was that what was keeping such a fresh impression of Matthew Saunders's face in her mind?

'It was quite hard for Russell at first, with the bond that Matt and Bonnie developed so quickly, but now we can appreciate the extra love she's getting. And Matt's been such a help as far as the medical side of things has gone. He's found the best specialists and explained everything. We've often rung him up in the middle of the night because we're worried about something and he's always happy to help. Getting to know him has been another aspect of adopting Bonnie that we'll always be grateful for. He's been just as excited as us about this pregnancy.' Karen patted her stomach gently. 'He's been helping Bonnie think up names for her new brother or sister.' She grinned. 'It's being called Piglet at present. Bonnie's a great fan of Pooh Bear. That's why Tigger is called Tigger. Matt gave her that toy years ago. It's been her cuddly ever since.'

Polly made a noncommittal sound. The picture of Matthew Saunders as a saint didn't quite gel.

'He didn't even know he had a child,' Karen said quietly. 'A lot of men would have run a mile from involvement like that.'

'It could play havoc with a marriage,' Polly agreed. 'Especially if he had other children.'

'Matt's never been married,' Karen informed her. 'Maybe Donna put him off.'

'Donna?'

'Bonnie's mother. She was a nurse. They were living together but it was months before he found out about her drug problems. She refused to try rehabilitation and took off when she was fired for stealing morphine. Matt traced her to try and persuade her to get help, but she made all sorts of threats if he didn't leave her alone so he gave up. He had no idea she was pregnant.'

'So how did he find out about Bonnie?'

'When Bonnie was first diagnosed with leukaemia, we discussed all the treatment options. The fact that she was adopted made it tricky because the oncologist wanted to know if she had any siblings in case a bone-marrow transplant was needed later. Russell and I talked about it a lot and decided that it was worth at least finding out. We hired a private detective to track Donna.'

'Did you find her?'

'We found out that she'd died from another drug

overdose about a year after Bonnie was born. The detective was thorough, though. He'd traced her employment records and had uncovered the information about who she'd been living with at the time she became pregnant. It seemed likely that Matt would be the father of the baby, and while a parent is only a half-match as far as being a donor goes, it was better than Russell or I could offer. We took the risk and made an approach to Matt. He had himself tested immediately and he's the best match we could have hoped for. We've been waiting and hoping for more than two years now that it wouldn't be needed, but it looks like it's finally going to go ahead.'

Polly had been absorbing the information with some dismay. So Matt hadn't given up his child. He hadn't known of her existence. And when he'd found out, he'd done all he could to help. He was probably about to undergo a fairly unpleasant medical procedure himself in the hope that it would provide a cure for Bonnie. More than a little revision of her opinion of this man was called for. Maybe even an apology, should she ever get the opportunity.

The opportunity arrived far sooner than Polly could have anticipated. Karen had been looking weary all day. The strain of being with Bonnie through two long procedures had taken its toll. When she came back from a trip to the toilet and informed Polly that she was bleeding, Polly felt almost as alarmed as Karen now looked.

'How far are you along in your pregnancy?'

'Just over twenty weeks.'

'Have you had any problems with bleeding before?'

'A bit, but nothing like my previous pregnancies.'

Karen's face was very pale. 'I couldn't bear it if something went wrong now. Bonnie's so excited about this baby.' Karen was fighting back tears. 'We thought it would give her something to look forward to while we all get through this lot of treatment.'

'We don't know that anything's going wrong,' Polly said calmly. 'What we need to do is get you and the baby checked out. I'll make some calls. When is Russell coming in again?'

'He should be here any minute.'

'Good. He'll be able to go with you to the gynaecology department.'

'But who will stay with Bonnie?'

'I will.'

'Aren't you due to go off duty?'

'That doesn't matter. In fact, it's good.' Polly smiled encouragingly. 'I can stay with Bonnie and I won't be called away for anything else.'

The only calls away in the next few hours were those dictated by nature—a quick trip to the toilet and a slightly longer one to the cafeteria. Bonnie had woken briefly between Polly's absences. She hadn't seemed unduly bothered to find her parents missing.

'Will you read me a story, Polly?'

'I'll read as many stories as you like, sweetheart,' Polly promised.

'I want the one about the tiger. The one that doesn't like the dark.'

'Sure. How about we give you a quick wash and make you comfy first? I need to do that nurse stuff and take your pulse and things, too. Do you want me to get you anything to eat?'

'No. My tummy's sore.'

'Is it, pet?' Polly's brow creased. Bonnie often had

to contend with abdominal pain due to an enlarged liver and spleen. She made a quick call to an oncology registrar to check the pain-relief protocol for Bonnie.

The additional dose of pain relief was probably responsible for Bonnie falling asleep again before the story was finished. With Stephanie now available to come and sit with Bonnie for a while, Polly took the break to find something to eat. The cafeteria shut at 9 p.m. and she would be lucky if there was anything remotely enticing left by now. When she returned, carrying a bag of fairly sad sandwiches, Polly was surprised to find Stephanie outside the ward office. Her friend raised her eyebrows.

'I got kicked out,' she told Polly. 'Bonnie's got someone else sitting with her. You'll never believe who it is. Matthew Saunders—the surgeon.'

Polly nodded. 'He's a family friend.' She wasn't about to share any more information. 'I'd better go and see if he needs to get away.'

She opened the door to Bonnie's room very quietly, not wanting to disturb her if she was sleeping. Matt seemed unaware of her entrance and Polly stopped still. She swallowed hard. He was holding one of Bonnie's hands. He was gazing at the child's face with an expression of real pain…and he had tears rolling down his cheeks.

Polly knew she stood step away and give him a moment of privacy but she was transfixed. The empathy she felt was overwhelming. More than a few tears of her own had been shed in solitary times over the last few days. Russell and Karen Weaver were wonderful people and they had a marriage that anyone would envy. All they had ever wanted was to raise their own family and share the love they so obviously had for each other. This was just so unfair. For Bonnie and all the people who loved her. Including her birth father. And including Polly herself. She had to blink hard to clear accumulating moisture from her own eyes. She swallowed and was then forced to sniff. Matt turned away at the sound, taking a moment to compose his features. The glance Polly received, however, was still touchingly vulnerable.

'Hi,' Matt said softly. 'Bonnie's fine. She's been asleep ever since you left.'

Polly nodded. 'How's Karen doing?'

'She's OK. The ultrasound didn't show any abnormalities. She's been ordered to rest and they've admitted her overnight. She's totally exhausted.'

'Is Russell still with her?'

'For the moment. He's coming down here later.'

'He doesn't need to. I offered to stay with Bonnie tonight.'

'So I heard.' Matthew motioned to the chair beside him with his free hand. 'Sit down for a minute, would you, Polly?'

This was her opportunity. Polly sat, her heart thumping. Having summoned the courage to apologise, it was frustrating when they both spoke at the same time.

'I've been wanting—' Polly had begun.

'Karen tells me—' Matt had started.

They both stopped. And waited for the other to speak again. Finally they both smiled.

'You go ahead,' Matt invited.

'I just wanted to say I'm sorry.' It seemed easy now that she'd begun. 'I had no right to make any judgements about you or your relationship with

Bonnie. I'm sure you must have had a very good reason to tell me something so private and I never really gave you the chance to finish.'

'Would you like to know?'

Polly was looking at Bonnie. Her gaze caught the child's hand, still enclosed in Matt's. She saw the gentle stroke of the man's thumb across the tiny fingers. When she looked up to gain eye contact with Matt, Polly received a smile. A smile that was so poignant and so full of obvious love for the sleeping child that Polly dismissed any doubts she had harboured about this man's integrity.

'I would like to know. Very much,' she confirmed softly.

'If the worst happens,' Matt said carefully, 'then Karen and Russell want to have Bonnie at home with them. They're going to need a lot of help. I've been keeping an eye out for a special nurse who might be able to work privately in that kind of situation. Someone that Bonnie will trust.'

Polly nodded but private nursing wasn't something she had ever considered. It would be totally heartbreaking in this particular case.

'Hopefully, that's well into the future, if at all,' Matt continued. 'There was a more immediate reason for me taking you into my confidence.'

'Which is?'

'I have a trip planned to Brisbane. I'm speaking at a conference that's starting the day after tomorrow. I want to take Bonnie with me.'

'Isn't she too sick to travel?'

'She has an amazing ability to bounce back. These tests are knocking her at the moment.' Matt smiled. 'Have you noticed the passion Bonnie has for tigers?'

Polly returned the smile. 'It would be hard not to.'

'There's a tiger park at Dreamworld. I've looked into it. Bonnie could actually pat a tiger and play with the tiger cubs they have at the moment. It would be a dream come true for her.'

Polly nodded. Just the kind of special wish someone would want to make happen for a terminally ill child.

'It might be the last chance I ever get to spend some time with my daughter.'

Polly nodded again. What could she say?

'I couldn't do it by myself, however. Very few people know about Bonnie's parentage. I could have offered to take Karen and Russell with me, but I'm selfish enough to want a little time just for myself. It would be impossible now, in any case, with this worry about the pregnancy. In fact, it's the perfect time to give them both a few days' complete rest.' Matthew was watching Polly intently as he spoke. 'If I did take Bonnie with me. I would need help of a medical nature. Bonnie needs constant monitoring and she has a fairly extensive drug regime, as you must be well aware by now.'

'You want me to come to Brisbane with you?' Polly almost forgot to keep her voice down.

'With me and Bonnie. Just for a couple of days.'

'I have four days off, starting on Friday. Nobody would need to know where I was going. Would that be long enough?'

'It would be perfect. Do you mean you'll consider it?'

'I don't need to consider it.' Polly looked at the tiny face on the pillow beside them. Dark lashes feathered pale cheeks and the downward slant of

Bonnie's mouth gave her an uncharacteristically sad expression. Polly could well imagine the joy the little girl would experience from the surprise her Uncle Matt was planning. She wanted to be there to share that joy. She looked up at Matt and held his gaze with confidence.

'I'm quite sure about this,' she told him. 'I'd love to come to Brisbane with you.'

CHAPTER THREE

'ALL set to go, then?'

Polly's affirmation was a silent nod. She was momentarily disconcerted by the appearance of the man who had just entered the hotel room she was sharing with Bonnie. The pinstriped suit she associated with Matt at work was gone, although he had been wearing it only this morning to attend the medical conference. She had assumed the sports jacket and linen trousers worn for the flight to Brisbane yesterday had been a conservative man's casual gear, but now he had surprised her again. Soft-looking corduroy trousers, casual shoes and a short-sleeved, open-necked shirt made the surgeon look as though he intended to have fun.

'Where are we going?' Bonnie demanded.

'Not telling.' Matt's tone was firm. He leaned down to pick Bonnie up in his arms. 'It's a surprise.'

Maybe it wasn't the clothing that was making Matt look so different. Maybe it was the gleam of anticipation that made his face appear animated and gave those dark brown eyes a distinct gleam of…mischief? Polly knew she was staring. Boring men, even those with secrets—especially those with secrets—were never mischievous. Her curious gaze was acknowledged with a raised eyebrow.

'All set?' Matt repeated.

Polly nodded again. 'All set,' she replied confidently. She picked up the pillow and blanket she was taking in case Bonnie needed to sleep in the car Matt had hired. The tote bag was stuffed with extra clothes in case Bonnie got cold despite the mild day. There was sunscreen to protect Bonnie's pale skin and a sunhat to cover a scalp overly exposed by the sparse hair. The hat would also have the extra benefit of preventing intrusive stares from strangers. A small plastic box contained medications—pain relief and anti-nausea drugs mainly, but Polly even had a thermometer and a loading dose of antibiotics available in case Bonnie started running a temperature. With an immune-depressed condition, even a few hours was too long to allow an infection to gain ground. Polly was here as a nurse and she intended to fulfil her role as professionally, albeit unobtrusively, as possible.

It was simply professionalism that prompted the glance into the long mirror near the door of the hotel suite. The gaze Polly saw in the dark blue eyes staring back at her was querying how Matt might view her appearance. Did it matter that she hadn't tied her hair back in a ponytail—as she always did at work? That she had applied a little more make-up than she usually did? Were her very casual clothes of well-worn jeans and the close fitting T-shirt acceptable? The glance was very brief. It was too late to worry now and it was her professional qualifications that were important here after all.

So why did it feel like a family outing, once they were all settled in the car and travelling south from Brisbane down the Gold Coast motorway? Matt negotiated the route out of the city with minimal help from Polly, who sat in the front passenger seat with a map spread open on her lap. Bonnie was strapped into her booster seat in the back with Tigger firmly clutched in her arms.

Maybe it was the game of Twenty Questions Matt was playing with his daughter.

'Is it bigger than a breadbin?'

'No.'

'Is it alive?'

'Hmm.' Matt had to think about that one. 'No,' he decided somewhat reluctantly.

'Have I got one?'

'Yes.'

'Is it inside the car?' Polly couldn't help contributing.

'Yes.' Matt's quick smile encouraged her participation in the game.

'Is it something to eat?' Bonnie queried.

'No.'

'Is it something to wear?'

'No.'

'Do I like it?'

'Oh, yes.' Matt slipped Polly the ghost of a wink. 'Your twenty questions must be nearly up by now, tuppence.'

'Um...' Bonnie was thinking hard. Polly stole a glance over her shoulder and hoped that the frown indicated concentration rather than any discomfort.

'Does it have whiskers?' Polly broke the pause.

'Yes.' Matt sounded surprised.

'Does it have a tail?' Polly suggested cunningly.

'It's *Tigger*!' Bonnie shouted happily.

'OK. It's your turn to pick something now, Bonnie.'

'No. I want a song. Sing something, Uncle Matt.'

He appeared to be concentrating on a lane change

but Polly could sense his embarrassment. Knowing a child's song, let alone singing one, would be a less-than-dignified activity for a consultant surgeon being accompanied by a professional colleague.

'Sing about the dragon,' Bonnie commanded. 'The magic one. Puff,' she added finally to clear up any confusion.

Polly almost held her breath, waiting to see how Matt was going to handle the request. Once again, he surprised her. Not only by his compliance but by the delightfully tuneful and rather poignant rendition of the old song. Bonnie had clearly heard it many times before. She joined in and piped lines about sealing wax, billowed sails and the dragon's fearful roar. Polly only knew the chorus. Matt looked surprised the first time she joined in. By the time the last verse was over they were all singing together as though it was the way they passed every car journey, and Polly couldn't remember when she had last enjoyed herself so much. It was almost disappointing to pull off the motorway into a reserved car park near the entrance to the huge theme park of Dreamworld.

They were expected. The visit had been arranged in advance down to the last detail and a welcoming official escorted the trio past the queues at the ticketing counters and into the park. Bonnie had fallen completely silent and was now looking even paler than normal. She was in Matt's arms again and her huge round eyes appeared almost glazed as she stared into the windows of the souvenir shop they were passing. A dazzling array of products were on display and they all appeared to be centred on tigers. Polly wondered anxiously whether the sheer excitement of this venture was going to prove too much for the sick child.

Matt was also taking in the window display. 'We'll find something to take home later,' he told Bonnie. Adjusting her weight against his hip, he had to catch the slipping strap of his camera bag and push it back into place on his shoulder. 'Right now, I think there's someone waiting to meet you.'

Their escort nodded. 'This is Tim—one of our handlers.'

The young man smiled warmly at Bonnie. 'Hey, princess. I hear you like tigers.'

Bonnie stared at Tim. A shy nod was promptly followed by hiding her face against Matt's shoulder.

'Have you ever patted a real, live tiger?'

Bonnie's eyes appeared again as she slowly shook her head.

'Well, you're going to today. If you want to, that is.' Tim was smiling again. 'They can be a bit scary when they're real but our Kamahl is just an oversized pussycat. A bit bigger than your friend, though.' Tim touched the toy in Bonnie's arms. 'What's his name?'

'Tigger.' Bonnie had decided she liked Tim. She finally returned his smile. 'I'm not scared. Polly says I'm as brave as a real tiger.'

'Cool. Let's go and find some, then.' Tim turned his attention briefly to Matt and Polly. 'I thought we'd start with the cubs,' he said. 'They're due for a feed in a few minutes.'

The three tiger cubs were only the size of large domestic cats but Polly felt nervous as Tim lifted the tiny and suddenly fragile-looking child into the cubs' pen. He noticed her expression.

'She'll be fine,' he reassured Polly. He crouched

beside Bonnie. 'Does your mum like tigers as much as you do?'

Bonnie didn't bother correcting Tim's assumption. She probably hadn't heard it. A cub was crawling groggily into her lap as the handler was speaking, and the other two sleepy babies were rousing themselves with soft mewing sounds and exaggerated stretches.

'They only opened their eyes a couple of days ago,' Tim told Bonnie. 'They can't see very well yet but they can smell the milk. I think they might be hungry, don't you?'

Bonnie still didn't speak. She had an armful of striped fur now and her cheek was pressed against the side of the cub's face. Polly had to blink away tears at the joy radiating from the child's dark eyes. Glancing at Matt to see how he was coping with Bonnie's ecstatic reaction, she found him apparently concentrating on adjusting a very professional-looking lens on his camera. He crouched beside the pen and started snapping pictures as Tim helped Bonnie position the bottle of milk and settle the eager cub into enjoying his meal. Bonnie looked up at Matt as the cub suckled and Polly knew that the smile his camera recorded would be reward enough for any effort this trip had taken.

Her own pleasure in being part of it increased as Tim placed a cub and bottle into her own arms.

'Here you go.' He grinned. 'You'll be good at this. It's not much different to a human baby.'

Tim wasn't to know that Bonnie wasn't her child. And Polly wasn't about to confess she had never bottle-fed any kind of baby before. Her nursing career had only just taken her into paediatrics and there had never been any call to feed babies in Theatre or emergency department work. This was a new experience, and the sensation of a tiny mouth tugging on the bottle's teat stirred something deep within Polly. The sense of nurturing was strong enough to prompt a totally unconscious smile that reflected the joy she felt. It wasn't until the click of the camera shutter close by made her glance up that Polly realised she *was* smiling, and then she found she couldn't stop. Her smile broadened as Matt lowered the camera until she caught the expression in his dark eyes. He recognised what she was feeling and he was sharing that joy.

The moment of connection created a very peculiar sensation. A sensation as new as the emotions stirred by feeding the cub. Indefinable. Important. And more than a little disturbing. The eye contact seemed difficult to break and Polly felt relieved as she looked down to find her task completed. She handed the cub back to Tim and concentrated on helping organise the move towards the next step on their afternoon's adventure but the feelings stayed with her even as they toured the main tiger enclosure. Polly had to make a real effort to absorb the information Tim was sharing enthusiastically.

'Tigers sleep for up to eighteen hours a day,' he told them. 'When they're awake they play and swim and eat and relax. My job as a handler means I'm usually in the enclosure with them all day long.'

Matt set Bonnie down gently in order to pick up his camera and snap a handler who had a fully grown tiger standing on its hind legs beside him. The tiger's paws were wrapped around his shoulders. Matt whistled quietly, shaking his head in admiration.

'How do you get them that tame?' Polly queried.

'They're trained, not tamed,' Tim corrected her. 'We have to work on establishing and maintaining trust, respect and affection.'

'Sounds like a good marriage,' Matt murmured. Polly watched as he changed a lens before slotting the camera back into its carry case with practised ease.

'That's a pretty flash camera,' she observed.

'Mmm.' Matt slung the bag over his shoulder and stooped to collect Bonnie. 'Photography's been a hobby of mine for a long time. Since high school, in fact. I was the official photographer for the school magazine.'

'You must be good at it.'

'Not bad,' Matt admitted modestly. He settled Bonnie in his arms and then grinned at Polly. 'Maybe I'll show you my portfolio some time.'

Polly returned the grin. 'You don't do etchings as well, do you?'

Matt chuckled but the innuendo prompted a pause just long enough for the implications to be acknowledged on both sides. If Matt felt as uncomfortable as Polly, he certainly didn't show it.

'Is the white tiger an albino?' he asked Tim.

'No. It's the result of a recessive gene,' the handler responded. 'Kind of the equivalent of a blond-haired, blue-eyed version of a gold tiger.'

'I like the yellow ones,' Bonnie declared. 'Like Tigger.'

'That's good,' Tim said. 'Because that's where we're going next. To have your photo taken with the biggest yellow tiger we've got.'

The photo shoot with the adult tiger was carefully stage-managed. The tiger, Kamahl, was already lying on a raised platform with a backdrop of a jungle scene and potted shrubs on either side. A chain tethered the huge animal unobtrusively and a second handler stood close by. A professional photographer had his equipment and lights set up and was ready to take charge of the session.

'We'll get some pictures with everybody together and then do some individual and combination shots,' he informed them.

Polly hadn't expected to be included. 'I'll just watch,' she told the photographer. 'I'm just—'

'Scared?' Matt's voice was a murmur that tickled her ear.

'No.' Polly knew she sounded unconvincing. She eyed the astonishingly large tiger and swallowed hard. The absence of even a wire fence made a powerful difference to the atmosphere. 'This is for Bonnie,' she reminded Matt quietly. 'And you. I'm just an extra. I'm not really part of all this.'

'Aren't you?' Matt's gaze reminded Polly of the connection she had experienced during the cub feeding. Again it seemed to go on for a significant length of time and it drew her deeper into the emotional pull the reasons for this trip evoked. She was as much a part of making a wish come true for a terminally ill child as he himself was. The bond Polly felt with the little girl made the fact that she was unrelated immaterial. The look Polly was receiving from Matt let her know that he recognised the depth of her involvement, even if she didn't want to acknowledge it.

'Let's get going,' the photographer urged. 'We only have a fifteen-minute time slot here.'

Polly made no further protest as she and Matt were

positioned behind Kamahl with Bonnie kneeling between them.

'You can pat his back,' Tim told them, 'but you mustn't touch his head or feet.'

The tiger's coat felt surprisingly coarse. Polly found her hand shaking a little as she stroked Kamahl. No wonder Bonnie was too nervous to touch the tiger. Matt took Bonnie's tiny hand and held it under his as they patted the tiger together. Bonnie's fingers caught at Polly's when they touched.

'Look up,' the photographer directed. 'Big smile, everyone!'

It was all over very quickly.

'I'll get these shots developed straight away. They'll be ready for you in less than an hour.' The photographic gear was already being packed away.

'Is there anything else you'd like to see?' Tim queried. 'You could have a photo taken cuddling a koala or feeding the kangaroos.'

'There's all the fun rides, too,' the other handler added. 'Roller-coasters and the train.' She was grinning at Matt. 'You look like you could even handle Terror Tower.'

'No.' Matt had Bonnie in his arms again. She lay quietly with her head pillowed on his shoulder, her eyes still huge in a pale face. 'I think we've done enough for today. We're going to have a look in the tiger shop and then go home for a sleep. Maybe we'll come back tomorrow to see the other animals.'

'Are you OK, sweetheart?' Polly leaned closer to Bonnie. 'Is anything sore?'

Bonnie shook her head. Her eyelids drifted shut as she smiled. Matt could feel the change in the weight of his burden.

'She's exhausted.' His frown betrayed his concern. 'Let's go and get her settled in the car. I think I'd better go shopping by myself.'

Polly strapped Bonnie into the booster seat and arranged the pillow and blanket for greatest comfort. Her patient remained soundly asleep and Polly carefully checked Bonnie's temperature, pulse and respiration rate, but could find no reason for real concern. Bonnie had had the adventure of a lifetime and the excitement had stretched her stamina. What she needed now was a good rest.

The photographs were ready to collect by the time Matt had finished making his purchases. He returned to the car laden with carrier bags and Polly was smiling as he loaded them into the boot of the car.

'You look like Santa Claus.'

Matt's smile was embarrassed. 'I won't give them to her all at once. I think she's had more than enough excitement for one day.' His face was sober as he climbed into the car. 'She's got a rough few weeks coming up in the bone-marrow transplant unit. A new surprise every few days or so might help.'

'Will they go ahead with the transplant, do you think?'

Matt paused for a moment before starting the car. He took a long glance at the sleeping child behind them. 'It's about the only real hope we've got,' he said quietly. 'I'm not a perfect match but it's going to be the closest there is available.'

'What does it involve for you?'

'It's no big deal.' Matt sounded casual as he eased the car back into the motorway traffic heading for Brisbane. 'An overnight stay in hospital, a general or epidural anaesthetic and a few puncture sites around the iliac crests. I'll be bouncing around as normal in a couple of days.' He threw Polly a speculative glance. 'Why are you smiling?'

'It sounds like quite a big deal to me,' Polly responded. 'Though I confess to being a wimp.' She hesitated briefly. 'And I guess the image of you ''bouncing around'' is not one that people would generally associate with Matt Saunders.'

Matt acknowledged the comment with a lopsided smile. 'I guess not. But most people don't know me very well. I've been very careful to keep my private life private.' He threw another glance towards the back seat. 'For obvious reasons. I imagine the general impression around the hospital is that I'm fairly antisocial. Conservative. Boring as hell, I expect.'

Polly couldn't help grinning. She was certainly learning her own lesson about judging books by their covers.

'So I'm right?' Matt's smile was rueful. 'Ah, well. Maybe I'll surprise everyone one of these days.'

'You've surprised me,' Polly admitted. 'I don't think you're boring at all.'

'I must say, I don't think you're boring either. In fact…' Matt took his eyes off the traffic for a fraction longer than wise '…I think you're possibly the most interesting person I've ever met.'

Polly's laugh disguised the pleasurable thrill that Matt's words generated. 'You don't know anything about me!'

'So tell me,' Matt commanded. 'Fair's fair. You know a lot about me.'

'There's nothing much to tell.' Polly felt suddenly shy. She liked the idea that Matt found her interesting.

She liked it rather a lot. 'In fact, I suspect I'm quite genuinely boring.'

They both laughed. The sound was enough to make Bonnie stir in the back seat and Polly turned to take the child's hand. Bonnie didn't wake up completely but Polly kept hold of her hand.

'She feels quite warm,' she told Matt. 'And her heart rate's up a bit. It's 96. Do you think she might be running a temperature?'

'We'll give her a proper check when we get back to the hotel. It's less than an hour away and she's better off resting right now. If there's any hint of her being unwell later we'll bring our flights forward and get back to Christchurch tonight or tomorrow morning.' Matt changed lanes and accelerated to clear a line of slower-moving traffic.

'So, tell me.' Matt's repetition came after a companionable silence. 'I want to know how boring your life is. What do you do when you're not working?'

'I used to travel a lot,' Polly told him. 'It was partly why I went into nursing in the first place. It's a very transportable career and I've never had trouble getting jobs overseas. I based myself in England for five years while I explored as much of the world as I could. I'd work for a few months and then spend all the money I'd saved on travelling. By the time I came back here a year ago I was completely broke and probably cured of my itchy feet.'

'Did you travel alone?'

'Not for the last couple of years.' Polly took a deep breath. She hadn't told any of her colleagues the real reason she had returned to New Zealand. 'I lived with a guy who was a presenter for a television travel show. I went on location with him whenever I could.'

Polly tried to sound offhand. 'We went to some amazing places. The Bahamas and Africa. Peru, even.'

'Hmm.' Matt sounded politely impressed. 'Did he come back to Christchurch with you, then?'

'No.' Polly stared straight ahead through the windscreen. 'He went back to his wife instead.'

'Oh.' The silence seemed to reverberate with the information that Polly was unattached, having been dumped, but the glance she received conveyed understanding rather than sympathy.

'Kind of puts you off, doesn't it?' Matt suggested. 'When things go badly wrong?'

'Mmm.' Polly couldn't help casting another glance towards the sleeping child in the back seat as she remembered what Karen had said about Bonnie's mother and the effect the relationship had had on Matt. But that was more than five years ago. Surely he had had other women in his life since then?

Matt had noted the direction of her glance. 'I know how much Karen told you about Bonnie's mother,' he said. 'She wanted to check that I didn't mind.'

'And did you?'

'No. Karen said she told you because she felt that you were completely trustworthy.' Matt's tone was serious. 'And I said that was the way I felt as well.' He smiled slowly. 'I knew I could trust you right from the moment I saw you up that tree, holding Bonnie in your arms.' Holding his daughter. Matt still hadn't even tried to define how that had made him feel. 'Mind you, I thought I'd made a terrible mistake when you reacted the way you did to the news that I was Bonnie's father.'

'I *was* shocked,' Polly admitted. 'But then I had no idea of the background.' She smiled. 'And your reputation hadn't given me any basis to expect a surprise like that.'

'Not a boring thing to tell someone, was it?'

Polly was still smiling as she stole another glance at Matt's profile. He was smiling as well. She loved the way the corners of his mouth curled up so distinctively, creating that single dimple on the left side. Fascinating that a genetic quirk like that could be passed on. It was an interesting quirk. Definitely not boring.

Polly had to work on suppressing her smile before it began to seem inappropriate. It was a private joke now that Matt could be considered boring. But it could only have become a joke because Matt knew quite well that she did not find him boring. In fact, if he was half as sensitive as Polly suspected he might be, he probably had a very good idea of just how attracted she now was. Help. Polly cleared her throat.

'What's the programme for Bonnie once we get her back to Christchurch?'

Matt accepted the change of topic smoothly. 'Karen should be discharged today so Bonnie can have a night or two at home then she'll be admitted to the unit, have a central venous line inserted and then undergo a few days of chemotherapy and radiation which will destroy her own bone marrow. After that she gets the transplant and then comes the hard part. Weeks and weeks of waiting. Blood transfusions and antibiotics and worry about preventing and fighting any infection. She'll be isolated from all but a few visitors.' Matt glanced at Polly. 'We'll have to make sure you're on the list.'

'I'd like that.' Polly nodded. 'I'm just sorry I won't

be able to nurse her. It's going to be a tough time for everyone.'

'Karen and Russell will need a lot of support,' Matt agreed.

So will you, Polly added silently. Maybe she could be there for Matt as well. Bonnie had brought them together. Maybe now she was going to give them the opportunity to get even closer.

'They'll really appreciate any involvement you want to have,' Matt continued. 'They really like you, Polly.'

'I like them, too,' Polly responded. 'And Bonnie would win anyone's heart. She's an amazing little girl.'

'You're pretty amazing yourself, Polly Martin.' Matt spoke quietly, having pulled the car to a halt outside their hotel. He unclipped his safety belt, leaning slightly towards Polly as he did so. 'Maybe I should warn you now...'

'Warn me?' Polly bit her lip. Was the prognosis for Bonnie even worse than she feared? 'What do you need to warn me about?'

'Me.' The gaze from those dark eyes was very serious. 'I don't want to scare you off, Polly but I should warn you that I find myself very, very attracted to you.'

'Oh-h.' Relief and pleasure mingled to send a warm flush of colour to Polly's cheeks. She glanced down as she unclipped her own seat belt. 'Thanks for the warning,' she said sombrely. She caught Matt's gaze again just as the hotel's parking valet opened her door.

'I'm not scared,' she added softly. She smiled. 'Not even a little bit.'

CHAPTER FOUR

POLLY was scared.

Very scared.

She sat in the waiting area near the theatre suite on the first floor, watching the minute hand crawl around the face of the wall clock again. And again. How could time be moving so slowly? And how could she feel so strongly about the welfare of a man she'd met only two weeks ago? A man who was due to emerge from one of the operating theatres any minute now.

The waiting time had so far been passed by Polly trying to convince herself that she was not worried. Matt wasn't having a general anaesthetic with its small but significant associated risk. An epidural was quite enough for the procedure of harvesting bone marrow and it was quite possible that Matt was enjoying himself, conversing and even exchanging jokes with his colleagues. Polly had to confess that part of her anxiety was simply due to the fact that she would have preferred to be with him, but it had been too soon to suggest sharing an experience that personal. It was certainly far too soon for a man as private as Matthew Saunders to want to go public with his new relationship.

It was a relationship now. It had been ever since the night they had returned with Bonnie from Brisbane. Russell and Karen had noticed something within minutes of them dropping Bonnie home from the airport. Polly had been surprised by the significant glance that passed between the couple. It wasn't as though she and Matt had done anything more than acknowledge their attraction to each other so far. Polly would have liked to have assured the Weavers that they wouldn't have considered doing anything more—not with Bonnie in their care—but any inference that had been made based on her interaction with Matt had been clearly forgotten after Bonnie had been settled in her bed and Matt had brandished the package of photographs taken at Tiger Island. The distraction had been more than enough of a diversion.

The professional photographer had done his job superbly. While the backdrop and potted shrubs had seemed artificial at the time, the photographs made them look as though they were sitting in a patch of jungle, having encountered a very co-operative wild animal. The package deal included some enlargements, one of which had been beautifully framed. The picture they had chosen for this treatment was one of the whole group. It must have been one of the earlier shots in the sitting, when Matt had held Bonnie's hand to encourage her to stroke the tiger. Bonnie's fingers had caught Polly's just as the photographer had asked them to look at the camera. The result was all he could have wished for. Even Kamahl had looked straight ahead. Polly and Matt were sitting sideways with Bonnie kneeling between them and their hands were all linked as they rested on the back of the tiger. Matt looked a little serious, Polly looked a little nervous but Bonnie's wide smile and huge eyes shone with absolute ecstasy.

Russell had to clear his throat and Karen's eyes filled with tears.

'She looks *so* happy,' Karen whispered brokenly. 'I wish I could have been there.'

'We'll get another chance,' Russell comforted her. 'When Bonnie's well enough not to need a medical escort.' He smiled at his wife. 'And when we feel strong enough to travel with two children in tow.'

Karen nodded as she blew her nose, accepting Russell's optimism, but the glance she shared with Matt acknowledged the fear she was trying so hard to conceal. Polly could sense the empathy Matt was experiencing even before he hugged Karen.

'Thanks *so* much, Matt,' she heard Karen whisper. 'It was a magic thing to do.'

Russell was nodding now. He reached out to rub Karen's shoulder and Polly was aware of the unusual bond between these people. A shared love for a sick child that created a unique group that she now felt very much a part of. That she wanted very strongly to be a part of.

'I couldn't have managed without Polly,' Matt said.

Then it was Polly's turn to be hugged and she really did feel part of the group. Bound to Bonnie and her parents, her adoptive parents, and most particularly to her natural father. Matt was watching her now, his expression unreadable.

'I'll have heaps more photos,' he told the Weavers. 'You haven't seen any of the cub-feeding ones yet. We dropped all the films into a pharmacy on the way here. We'll collect them on the way home.'

It was unsurprising that Matt's choice of words made the Weavers exchange another private glance. Polly had wondered herself whose home he might have been referring to.

It wasn't Polly's flat they'd headed towards, having

collected the packets of photographs. She found herself being driven to Matt's address, having agreed readily to his suggestion of a coffee and a sneak preview of the pictures.

There were a lot of photographs to admire. The coffee led to a glass of wine. A quick tour of the penthouse apartment followed, and Polly was very impressed by the taste Matt displayed in his choice of home and furnishings. The apartment was spacious and had a very Mediterranean feel with tiled floors and colourful rugs. The furniture had deceptively simple lines. Polly knew quite well that comfort levels like that didn't come cheaply. The boys' toys like state-of-the-art audio-visual equipment that she might have expected a wealthy bachelor to have accumulated were discreetly concealed, if there at all. There were a lot of books and Matt's office had a sophisticated computer set up and floor-to-ceiling bookshelves filled with journals and textbooks. It was the room of a man who took his work very seriously and Polly was unsurprised that it was meticulously tidy.

Then Matt unpacked the souvenirs he had purchased at Dreamworld. Polly had agreed that the skullcap with the ears and the T-shirts looked a perfect size, that the drink bottle with the tiger's head would be useful and that the colouring-in books and crayons might help ease the boredom of a long hospital confinement. The book about tigers would be treasured and the tiger's paw slippers with long felt claws were the best choice of all.

'She'll absolutely love these!' Polly exclaimed. 'I wouldn't mind wearing them myself!'

'I hope they fit. I chose them in rather a hurry.'

The bottle of wine was almost empty by the time they picked out the best photographs to give Bonnie.

'I'll get this one enlarged.' Matt put the picture to one side. Bonnie's tiny arms made the cub look enormous. An oversized paw was keeping the bottle of milk in place and Bonnie was beaming at the camera.

'And this one...' Matt pulled another picture from the pile covering the coffee-table '...I'm going to keep for myself.'

Polly bit her lip, feeling a flush of colour creep into her cheeks. She wanted a copy of the shot Matt had taken when she had been feeding her cub. Matt had caught an expression she'd never seen on herself. A wistful smile and a dreamy gaze that made her look far better than anything a mirror had ever revealed.

'It's a lovely picture,' she murmured.

'It had a lovely subject,' Matt responded. His intent gaze caused the colour in Polly's cheeks to deepen further. When he reached out and stroked a gentle finger against her face she closed her eyes. The piles of intended gifts and photographs were forgotten as the sensation the touch generated spiralled throughout Polly's body. She opened her eyes to find Matt's face closer to her own. She kept her eyes open only to savour the building excitement as the gap closed. She wasn't sure if it was Matt moving his head or whether she was leaning closer. It made no difference the instant their lips touched.

It was the briefest contact, interrupted just long enough for them to pull back and gauge the reaction on each other with a searching gaze. The answer was there for them both and Polly closed her eyes firmly with the resumption of the kiss. Her hands reached for Matt's neck, her fingers slid into the soft waves of his hair, her lips and tongue responding with a rising passion to the rapidly deepening exchange. That they ended up making love on the first occasion they were genuinely alone seemed as natural as the way their bodies fitted together.

Nothing before had ever been as good as that time together, and Polly knew that no future encounter could ever match that experience of discovering just how wonderful it was possible for sex to be. She believed that for a full twenty-four hours, until the second time she and Matt made love, and it was even better than the first. Matt seemed to be as enthralled as she was herself. They spent all their free time together over the next few days. They went out for meals in restaurants and Matt visited Polly's tiny third-floor flat in an inner city complex, but more and more they were drawn to the privacy and comfort of Matt's apartment.

Polly's life was already centred on those times. Centred on Matt. It was no wonder she was feeling so anxious as she waited for him now. The anxiety was not simply that they were apart. What fed Polly's fear was the thought that Matt might not feel the same way. She knew he found the sex as unbelievable as she did—he had said as much on more than one occasion. Matt seemed as keen as she was to spend time together but what man wouldn't if the sex was that good? Matt hadn't wanted her to be with him during this procedure. He hadn't wanted to acknowledge their relationship publicly. Maybe the next couple of days when Matt wouldn't be in any condition to make love might be rather revealing as far as his feelings towards her went.

* * *

Matt could feel the pressure of the wide-bore needle entering his bones to suck out what seemed like huge quantities of bone marrow. The thick red fluid was drawn out a syringeful at a time. More than two litres had already been collected but Matt knew it represented only a small percentage of bone marrow that his body would replenish within a few weeks. The procedure was nearly finished now but it had been time-consuming. Had Polly bothered to wait for him? Matt found it had been possible to distract himself completely from the procedure he was undergoing by thinking about Polly.

It was unbelievable how good it felt being with her. It wasn't just the sex, as mind-blowingly amazing as it continued to be. It wasn't just her looks, although she was an extremely attractive young woman with that thick, soft golden hair, the dark blue eyes, that delicate straight nose that made her smile seem very wide. It was the smile he liked most and it appeared often. Polly was a happy soul and she smiled a lot. He loved just being in her company. Eating a meal, visiting Bonnie—even his professional encounters with patients took on a whole new enjoyment when Polly happened to be their nurse. He wanted to say something but hadn't found the moment. Or the courage.

It was too soon to expect Polly to feel anything like the same way. Too soon to expect her to want to be publicly associated with someone considered by most to be conservative and dull. Matt was trying very hard to take this whole relationship slowly. If he admitted how important it was then he would make himself vulnerable and, thanks to Donna, he had sworn never to do that again. At least not until he was absolutely sure that she felt the same way.

The look of relief that gave extra depth to those now familiar blue eyes was almost enough to convince Matt to say something the minute she came into the recovery room, but a nurse was hovering, taking his blood pressure, so he simply smiled instead.

'How was it?'

'No big deal,' Matt said. 'The epidural should wear off completely soon and then I'll be able to go home.'

'Aren't you supposed to stay in hospital overnight?'

'I have no intention of staying here that long.'

'Doctors make the worst patients.' Polly shook her head. 'They should insist on keeping you in.'

'They did.' Matt smiled. 'Until I told them I'd have someone medically qualified keeping an eye on me.'

'Oh?' Polly's look of surprise became a smile. 'Did you have someone particular in mind for this duty?'

'Of course.'

'A stern, matronly type who will make sure you behave yourself?'

Matt nodded. 'That's just the description I would have used. Mind you, I haven't checked that she's available yet.'

'I'm sure she is.' Polly kept a straight face. 'Stern, matronly types don't have much of a social life as a rule.'

'It will be an overnight duty,' Matt continued.

'I don't expect that will be a problem.'

'And I haven't got a spare bed.' Matt's smile could only be described as wicked.

'She'll manage,' Polly assured him very sternly.

'And there's no question of you doing anything other than resting.'

It was the first night in a week that they had not made love. It was also the first time Polly had stayed in Matt's apartment for a full night. A night without passion but with something Polly found just as satisfying. She stayed awake for a long time, with the weight of Matt's head on her arm. He was deeply asleep, thanks to the painkillers on top of a stressful day. Every so often, Polly reached out her other hand, to stroke his hair or touch his face very gently. She couldn't imagine not being here with him. Not just because he needed someone around right now but because she didn't want to be anywhere else. Or with anyone else. She was seriously in love with this man.

Matt woke to feel Polly's arm cradling him. He could hear the soft sigh of her breathing and was aware of the push of her breast on his arm as her chest rose with each breath. The incredible sense of contentment was not an emotion Matt would have expected to encounter on waking to find a beautiful woman in his bed. It was not something he'd ever felt before, although hints of it had been appearing ever since he'd met Polly. A feeling that this was it. He could give up ever worrying about what he might have missed out on in life because now he'd found it. It was part of his life. If only he could wake up beside this woman every day for the rest of his life, he would die a very contented man.

The contentment was being pushed aside right now, however. A more familiar sensation was gaining ground. An excitement that even a week of exploration and very enjoyable memories hadn't begun to quench. In fact, his desire only seemed to increase. He had to move his hips before his physical discomfort increased any more but the movement brought an unexpected distraction.

'Oh, hell!' Matt had almost forgotten that he'd spent yesterday afternoon having litres of bone marrow sucked out of multiple puncture sites over each hip. Now he felt like he'd been kicked by a very large horse. His groan had woken Polly instantly.

'What is it, Matt? What's wrong?'

'Nothing much.' Matt tried to sound reassuring. 'I'm just a bit stiff.'

Polly grinned. 'I noticed.' She sighed sadly. 'I doubt that you're really up to it, though.'

'Part of me is.' Matt groaned again and tried to move his hips to defuse his reaction to the touch of her body. 'Maybe having you look after me wasn't such a good idea after all.'

'I think it was an excellent idea,' Polly said. 'I'm going to make you a cup of tea and get you some more painkillers. Then you can have a nice long, hot shower.' She looked back over her shoulder as she climbed out of bed. 'You have the day off,' she added. 'And I don't start work until this afternoon. I suspect we can cure you before then, don't you?'

'I'm cured already.' Matt couldn't take his eyes off Polly as she covered herself with his bathrobe. 'Come back to bed, woman.'

The painful aftermath of the harvest procedure was soon forgotten. Matt would have gone through it a dozen times if it could have guaranteed a successful result for Bonnie. His daughter had been admitted to the bone-marrow transplant unit just a few days after her return from Australia. She had her own room, large enough for a second bed. Toys and games had been carefully cleaned before being installed in the room and fresh fruits, plants and flowers were banned due to the risk of imported fungi and bacteria. Precautions against exposure to infection began even before the conditioning process to destroy Bonnie's own bone marrow and thereby cripple her immune system. Polly was delighted to find herself on an exclusive list of permitted visitors. Often, she and Matt visited together and she was able to share in the pleasure he gained in delivering the presents he'd accumulated in Brisbane.

The skullcap with the tiger's ears was presented after the first procedure Bonnie had to undergo following admission when a central venous line had been inserted under general anaesthesia. This device was intended to remove the unpleasantness of multiple injections. Any drugs, fluids or blood products could be given and blood samples taken without the risk of a line tissuing and needing replacement. The risk of infection from repeated punctures was also lessened. Unfortunately, it was only one unpleasantness that could be dealt with. The chemotherapy had side effects that were difficult to control and other procedures were frightening if not painful.

Matt gave Bonnie the tiger slippers after her first session of radiation to augment the chemical destruction of her bone marrow. When Polly visited later that day she found Bonnie lying on her bed, grinning.

'I'm a tiger.'

'You sure are.' Polly smiled at the skullcap, the tiger pyjamas and the striped slippers with claws. She sat on the side of the bed. Bonnie seemed undeterred by her uniform of a gown and mask, climbing onto Polly's lap for a cuddle.

'How are you feeling, chicken?'

'I throwed up,' Bonnie told her. '*Six* times.'

'Oh, no!' Polly caught Karen's eye and Bonnie's mother nodded a little grimly.

'The chemo's obviously having an effect. They've added in some anti-nausea stuff now and she hasn't been sick for a couple of hours so here's hoping.'

'How are *you* feeling?'

'I'm coping.' Karen smiled. 'I had another check from my obstetrician this morning and he says everything's fine. I've just got to make sure I get enough rest. Matt and Russell are making me go home every night to sleep so that's helping.'

Polly nodded. She knew about the nightly vigils and intended sharing them with Matt whenever possible to give Russell some time at home with his wife.

After the bone-marrow transplant it was a matter of constant monitoring, treating any complications, protecting Bonnie from possible infection and waiting to see whether the donated bone marrow would 'take'. It meant weeks of an emotional roller-coaster that affected Matt and Polly as much as Karen and Russell. Bonnie would feel quite well one day but be tired and sick the next. She would spike a temperature and the results of blood tests would be anxiously awaited. Blood transfusions were done on a regular basis and signs of host-versus-graft disease carefully watched for.

Polly spent a lot of time in the unit on her days off. Often Karen was grateful for the opportunity to go outside for some fresh air or just put her feet up and rest. Her pregnancy was approaching a point where the extra weight she carried made her tire very easily on top of the stress of helping to care for Bonnie. While her work on the paediatric ward was enjoyable, Polly often found herself watching the clock, looking forward to finishing her duty and spending more time with Bonnie. And Matt. The hours they spent together in Bonnie's room were precious.

Sometimes Bonnie was awake and feeling well enough to delight in their company.

'Read to me,' she would command. 'The book about tigers.'

Although it was nothing like a story, Bonnie was never content to simply look at the pictures. 'Read the words, Uncle Matt,' she would insist.

'"Tigers are fully grown at two to three years of age,"' Matt read. '"Male cats can reach weights of two to three hundred kilograms and up to three metres in length. They have a white spot on the back of both ears to trick predators into thinking they are being watched."'

Sometimes Bonnie was asleep and those hours were special as well. Matt and Polly would sit beside her bed and converse quietly. It gave them opportunities to learn about each other, to share their histories, their ideas and their dreams. When Russell came in late in the evening to sleep in Bonnie's room, they would go home to Matt's apartment and the joyful continuation of the physical conversation they never seemed to tire of.

Each shared crisis and celebration brought them closer together and Polly couldn't believe how fast the weeks were slipping past. Or how much her life had changed, until her friend Stephanie confronted her prior to a staff handover one morning.

'Helen says she hasn't seen you for weeks.' It had been Helen who had introduced Polly to Stephanie and it had been Stephanie who had convinced Polly to make the change to the paediatric ward. Polly realised just how much she had neglected all her friends from the emergency department and felt guilty. The guilt increased as Stephanie kept talking.

'Helen says she's been trying to ring you at home. She wants to know if you're still planning to move into her flat when your lease expires.'

Polly hadn't been home long enough to check her answering machine for days.

'When *does* your lease expire?'

'Next month.' Having not known anyone in Christchurch on her return to New Zealand, Polly had taken a year's lease on the small one-bedroomed apartment near the hospital.

Stephanie was still chattering as the other staff gathered for the handover. 'If you don't want to move in with Helen's crowd, you'd better let her know 'cos there's a rather cute houseman in ED that's looking for a place. Do you know David Crew? I think he started the same week you left.'

'I remember. He is cute.'

'Mmm.' Stephanie was watching Polly's face. 'He was at the party last Saturday night. You know, the one you were supposed to come to?'

'Oh…sorry.' Polly bit her lip. 'I forgot about it.'

'Everyone was asking about you. The general consensus was that you've found a man.'

'Really?' Polly hoped her smile was enigmatic. She wasn't about to start any gossip that could get back to Matt. 'I'll give Helen a ring about the flat. I've still got a few weeks left on my lease and she won't want to keep a room empty if someone wants it.'

'What will you do if David moves in there, though?'

'I can find something else. Or stay where I am. I've got the option to renew my lease.'

'But aren't you lonely? Living all by yourself?'

Polly just smiled again. She had been lonely. She had been looking forward to moving to a vibrant houseful of young emergency department staff. Now she wasn't lonely at all. Even her hours by herself were filled with memories and dreams that kept her happy. More than happy. The way things were going between her and Matt it was probably only a matter of time before they were together on a permanent basis. After last Saturday night, Polly suspected that the amount of time might be rather short.

Thank goodness she had forgotten about the invitation to that party, otherwise she would have missed the most memorable night of her life. As Lee Fenton began the meeting by reviewing all current inpatients and their conditions, Polly found she was having difficulty concentrating. Snatches of that evening replayed themselves with too much pleasure to turn away.

The intimate restaurant in the beachside suburb of Sumner had been pleasant. So had the walk along the pathway above the beach back to the car, especially after Matt had taken her hand. Waves had been foaming over the rocks below them with muted strength. The sea had been calm and moonlight had gilded a pathway that had stretched enticingly towards the horizon.

Polly paused, pulling Matt to a stop. 'Look at that,' she breathed. 'Gorgeous, isn't it?'

'It is, indeed.'

Something in Matt's tone had made Polly glance up to find he was not looking anywhere near the seascape. Something inside her turned over at the intensity Matt's dark eyes revealed. She said nothing—acutely aware of what Matt might be about to tell her. The time it took was measured by the wild thumping of her heart against her ribs and in the end it was Polly who spoke, not Matt.

'I love you, Matt.'

Declaring her feelings first was the bravest thing Polly thought she'd ever done. How terrifying would it be if Matt said nothing back? For two heartbeats Matt didn't say anything but Polly's searching would have revealed any hint of fear or rejection in his eyes. What she saw, instead, was a sense of wonder. A surprise that was a very long way from being unpleasant. But it was clearly too soon for Matt to want to say anything back and it wasn't terrifying at all. The kiss more than made up for the silence. A long and passionate kiss left Polly in no doubt that Matt's feelings were just as strong as her own even if he was unwilling or unable to articulate them yet.

It took the prod of Stephanie's elbow to remind Polly where she was. Lee was giving her a strange look.

'You've got the new admission, Polly. Isaac Willis. A twenty-three-month-old who came in via ED two hours ago after a rectal bleed. He's waiting to be seen by the surgical registrar but they're still in Theatre with an emergency splenectomy that came in 3 a.m.'

Poor Matt, Polly thought. She hadn't left his apartment until after 1 a.m. He probably hadn't had any sleep at all.

'What's caused the bleeding?' Polly queried. 'Do they know?'

'They're querying a Meckel's diverticulum. I imagine they'll order a technetium scan before deciding whether surgery is indicated.' Lee was looking for Isaac's notes on her desk.

'What's a Meckel's diverticulum?' Stephanie whispered.

'It's the most common sort of gastrointestinal abnormality but it doesn't usually give any trouble.'

'In this case it has.' Lee gave Stephanie a disapproving glance. 'Isaac's mother went to change his nappy and found it full of bright red blood. The loss was significant and they started volume replacement in ED. A transfusion might be needed depending on the next blood results. He needs close monitoring, Polly. His mother is fairly anxious as well.'

Polly nodded. This could be an interesting case to special and with a bit of luck she would get to see Matt when he did his ward round. She tried to dismiss the surgeon from her thoughts as she headed onto the ward. Too much time had already been spent thinking about Matt since she'd left him last night. Polly was feeling a little jaded herself and the smell of the loaded nappy a nurse aide carried past her tinged her weariness with distinct nausea. She turned into the single room at the end of the corridor with relief that was short-lived.

'It's about time,' the woman snapped. 'We've been waiting for hours. How much longer is it going to be before we get to see a doctor?'

'The surgical registrar should be here soon,' Polly

told her calmly. 'They've been tied up with an emergency operation.'

'I would have thought this was an emergency.'

It was unsurprising that Isaac's mother was so anxious. The toddler looked pale and miserable. He was lying in his cot, crying weakly between attempts to pull the splint off the arm with the IV line in place.

'I'm Polly.' She smiled at the woman. 'I'm going to be Isaac's nurse today. You're his mum, aren't you?'

'Of course I am.' Isaac's mother gave Polly a look that suggested she was less than adequately intelligent. Then she sighed wearily. 'Sorry. I'm a bit tired.'

'It's OK,' Polly assured her. 'You're tired and you're worried. I understand.'

'My name's Sandra.'

'Hi, Sandra. As soon as I've checked Isaac I'll see about getting you a cup of tea. You look like you could use a break.'

'I'm just so worried. I couldn't believe it when I saw all the blood. Do you know what it might be? I'm sure it's cancer and they just don't want to tell me.'

'They'll tell you as soon as they know. Try not to worry too much.' Polly turned her attention to recording the toddler's vital signs, explaining everything she was doing to Sandra as she went along. Isaac's blood pressure was still low enough to be a concern.

'They said he might need a blood transfusion,' Sandra fretted.

'That will depend on the results of the blood tests,' Polly told her. 'A transfusion would probably make him feel a lot better than he does at the moment and it's nothing to worry about. I know a little girl who's having transfusions every few days.'

'What's wrong with her?'

'She's had a bone-marrow transplant to try and help treat her leukaemia.'

'Oh.' Isaac's mother was distracted from her own child's problems. 'That's really serious, isn't it?'

'It can be. We're hopeful that she's going to pull through. It's over a month now and she's doing really well.'

Later, Polly wondered whether her comment had tempted the fates. When the surgical team arrived to review Isaac Willis, Polly thought Matt looked more than just bone-weary. She grabbed the first opportunity she could to speak to him privately.

'Are you all right, Matt?'

'Tired,' he admitted. His smile looked strained. 'But you're looking a bit the same way.'

'I don't feel great,' Polly confessed.

'In what way?' Matt's weariness seemed to evaporate as he focussed on Polly.

'I just feel a bit off colour.' Polly shrugged. 'It's nothing serious. Maybe it was that chicken take-away we had last night.'

'Are there any cases of gastroenteritis on the ward here?'

'One or two...but I haven't been nursing them.'

'I imagine they have family members wandering around the ward.' The undercurrent of the conversation was suddenly disturbing. 'Bonnie was vomiting again this morning,' Matt continued evenly.

'Oh, no,' Polly groaned. 'Not again!'

'We're not sure if it's drug-related or a virus she's

picked up from somewhere.' Matt frowned. 'Maybe you'd better not come in to visit this evening.'

'You don't think *I've* passed something on, do you?' Polly was horrified. 'Even if I've been in contact with a bug, I was gowned and masked and scrubbed before I went into Bonnie's room.'

'I'm sure you haven't,' Matt reassured her. 'But it might be safer if you make sure you're OK before you come in again, that's all.'

'OK.' Polly hid her dismay. It was the time that she and Matt spent with each other—the visits to Bonnie. And then home to his apartment. If he thought she was sick, he wouldn't want contact with her himself in case he became a carrier. 'Let me know how she is,' Polly said forlornly. 'Ring me later.'

Matt rang late that evening. 'She's not looking great,' he reported. 'Her respiration rate is up to forty-five and the last blood test showed a deterioration of her renal function. How are you?'

The question seemed significant. Polly didn't want to tell Matt she'd felt too unwell to eat any dinner. 'I'm going to have an early night,' she said lightly. 'And knock whatever it is on the head. I'll be as right as rain by morning, I expect.'

But she wasn't as right as rain next morning. And neither was Bonnie.

'She's got respiratory distress,' Matt said flatly when he rang. 'They're wondering if she aspirated something when she was vomiting yesterday. The chest X-ray is OK but her temperature's up. How are you?'

Polly felt guilt-stricken. She had vomited herself that morning. Was she responsible for this new crisis? 'I'm starting two days off,' she told Matt. 'I'll get some rest and I've got an appointment with a doctor this afternoon.'

Worry about Bonnie made the day long and difficult. Polly knew that Matt, Karen and Russell would be gaining strength from each other as they battled through another tough day. She was an outsider again. Worse, she may have caused the dangerous situation.

She paged Matt late that afternoon. 'I don't have anything contagious,' she reported happily. 'And I'm feeling heaps better. I'll come in tonight.'

'No, don't do that.' Matt's tone was guarded. 'Visitors are being restricted to immediate family.' He was silent for a moment. 'Bonnie's not well enough to see you. She's been having multiple transfusions of packed red blood cells and platelets but her condition has deteriorated. She's got a high fever and the chest X-ray isn't looking good. They're considering transfer to the intensive care unit and ventilating her.'

'Oh, God.' Polly felt an icy chill envelop her. 'Is it that bad, Matt?'

The silence was even longer this time. 'It's that bad,' Matt said finally.

'Oh, Matt.' Polly was aching to be close enough to hold him. 'I wish I was there with you. Call me. Please?'

The telephone remained silent all night. Polly wanted to call Matt the following day. She debated whether or not to page him a hundred times.

No news is good news, she told herself. Matt will call when he has a chance.

It was so hard, not being there. She should be there. Even if she had no right to be near Bonnie at this time, surely Matt needed her. She needed him and if Polly felt this much in need of comfort herself, it had to be a totally unbearable situation for Matt. No matter how bleak the child's prognosis was, it was going to be heartbreaking for all concerned if Bonnie died. It might be harder on Matt than anyone else, in fact, when he couldn't acknowledge his relationship to his daughter. At least he knew now how much Polly loved him. She was there for him a thousand per cent. He would call her.

The telephone remained silent for yet another night.

'No news is good news,' Polly reminded herself as she arrived at the hospital early the next morning and headed straight for the bone-marrow transplant unit to ask for an update. The expression had become a kind of mantra during the long, sleepless night but the endless repetition hadn't made it any more believable.

Polly had the awful feeling she was stepping into a nightmare.

CHAPTER FIVE

IF ONLY it was all over.

The last few days had been unbearable but at least the emotional overload had led to an exhaustion that bestowed a manageable distancing effect. Matt felt curiously light-headed. Detached. Seeing himself from an observer's point of view gave him the hope that no one else in this gathering recognised that the dark suit and rigid self-control disguised a man whose spirit was shattered.

Thankfully the knowledge that he was Bonnie's father had never spread beyond the few trusted confidants. The reminder of the secret relationship brought an involuntary glance towards the tiny white casket which was accompanied by a fresh wave of pain that threatened to crack Matt's remote façade. It was the cap sitting amongst the flowers that was hardest to handle. A small, black and orange skullcap with rounded tiger's ears.

Maybe it would have been better if he'd never found out about the aftermath of that disastrous relationship with Donna. If only he'd had an inkling of what he had been letting himself in for three years ago when he'd agreed to meet Russell and Karen to discuss their adopted child. But it had never occurred to him that he might feel some kind of bond with the child. Or that the bond might flourish and develop into the first truly unconditional, selfless love of his adult life. Probably the only one he would ever have.

The fact that Donna had never intended him to know what a precious gift she had delivered had added immeasurably to the bitterness their broken relationship had seeded.

Would he rather not have known?

Matt listened to Russell and Karen as they stood bravely beside the casket, facing the large group of mourners. Hand in hand, with tears frequently interrupting and words often broken, they shared some of their memories of Bonnie. Excluding the adoption and the first two years of Bonnie's life, they were Matt's memories as well. They had shared so much since then. The worry about Bonnie's illness, the search for the best possible treatment, the many scares and setbacks they had weathered. They had also shared the joys. The times when it had seemed like they were going to win the battle against leukaemia, the milestones they had celebrated—birthdays, losing her first tooth, learning to tie her shoelaces. Each one all the more special because they had been bonuses. Poignant bonuses because they had all known the battle might very well not be won in the end. Funny how the expectation and even preparation for this eventuality had done nothing to dull the pain.

So much joy.

So much pain.

Thank God it was almost over. Soon they would be able to leave and then it might be possible to find a space where this wouldn't feel quite so much like the end of the world. If he could just hold himself together long enough then he might even to be able to survive all this.

* * *

It was almost over.

Polly had been sure that her body was incapable of producing any more tears but the music they played as the casket was carried away proved her wrong. Peter, Paul and Mary's rendition of 'Puff The Magic Dragon' left few dry eyes amongst the gathering. The band of paediatric nursing staff that surrounded Polly were crying openly. They had all come to know and love Bonnie during her many hospital admissions.

Although her vision was blurred by her own tears, the sight of Matt shocked Polly. He looked so pale. So remote. Could just a few days have made him lose enough weight to give his face such a haggard appearance? Polly blinked and stared anxiously as he walked past. No. The grim lines were due to the self-control Matt was exerting and it was simply his pallor that gave him an unshaven appearance. Polly's heart was breaking for him. She should have been standing beside Matt during this service, even if he did still want to keep their relationship off the hospital grapevine. She should have been with him over the few days since Bonnie's death. It had hurt so badly, this exclusion. Did Matt blame her for the complication that had led to Bonnie's death? If so, he would change his mind soon enough when he learned what the doctor had told her. A more distressing question was whether Bonnie had been the only link she had to that small group. Her only link to Matt.

No. Polly sniffed hard and waited her turn to move outside. Maybe Bonnie had been responsible for initiating the relationship but she and Matt had quickly stepped past those boundaries. And now there was a new link. One that would bind them together for a very long time. Polly's hand unconsciously touched her belly. There was real comfort to be found in the knowledge that Matt was going to be a father again. And this time he could be openly proud of it. He would be part of a family that would be genuinely his own.

It didn't matter that he hadn't told her yet that he loved her. Polly knew the truth. She had seen it in his eyes and felt it in that kiss on the beach. He had come so close to saying something. When he knew that Polly was carrying his child surely it would be enough to prompt him into revealing how he felt. Enough to start him rebuilding his life and looking to the future.

Right now was not the time to tell him, however much Polly had ached to do just that recently. It was a time for grief and she had had to respect Matt's request to be allowed his own space to deal with it. Maybe now, when the worst of the grieving was over, Matt would allow her close enough to offer some comfort. That was all she wanted for the moment. Any hint of what she knew the future held for them both would have to wait until she was sure Matt was ready.

Matt could see Polly moving towards him through the crowd of people. He watched as she stopped to hug Karen and Russell and share an obviously emotional conversation. He knew he shouldn't have asked her to stay away over the last few days. She should have been there to share the time they'd had Bonnie at home. Polly had loved the little girl. She had had every right to be there and the Weavers had been puzzled and hurt by her absence. It had been Matt who had kept her away and he had done it because he'd known he couldn't afford to indulge in the comfort she would have provided so willingly.

It was terrifying how close Matt had come to falling in love with this woman. How close he'd come to confessing it when they'd stood beside that moonlit sea. The words had been fortunately elusive but his body had almost betrayed him. He had been aware of the fleeting contact of their souls during that kiss and he had known that Polly was fast becoming more important than anything else in his life.

Even more important than his daughter had been.

Imagine if he'd gone any further down that track. If he'd acknowledged those feelings with anything more than that kiss, they would have grown. Become uncontrollable. And then what? What if Polly deceived and rejected him the way Donna had? What if Polly developed a terminal illness like Bonnie had? How could anyone willingly put themselves in danger of having to deal with such a devastating loss? Matt couldn't do this again. He *wouldn't* do it again. It felt too hard to survive as it was.

The voice alongside Matt forced him to turn his thoughts outward. The paediatric charge nurse, Lee Fenton, was saying something about how much the staff were going to miss seeing Bonnie's smile. Matt merely nodded.

'You knew her very well, didn't you?' Lee's tone was unusually soft. Sympathetic.

Matt cleared his throat. 'Karen and Russell are old friends and, yes…it was hard not to love Bonnie.'

He had to look away. It was too hard seeing his own pain reflected in the faces of others. Too intrusive to feel their desire to reach out and touch his soul. A soul that was too damaged and painful to tolerate even a stranger's light touch right now. The raw, bleeding wound needed covering in order to heal, and the less it was poked and prodded the faster that was likely to happen. That meant making an effort not to uncover it himself and it meant staying away from anyone who had access he would be powerless to prevent. People like Russell and Karen. And Polly. Especially Polly.

She was much closer now. Lee had sensed that her approach wasn't welcome and had melted into the crowd. Matt hadn't seen the black skirt and boots Polly was wearing. Had she chosen the burnt orange top deliberately to give herself the colours of a tiger? Matt tried to clamp down the memory but it was impossible. He couldn't even think of Polly now without remembering her sitting in that tree. Holding Bonnie. Or seeing an image of that framed photograph of the three of them patting Kamahl. The link was inextricable. And unbearable. That photograph had to go and, as hard as it might be, Polly would also have to go. It would hurt her. Of course it would. But it was a pain she would recover from—nothing like the kind of agony that made his own survival seem doubtful right now.

'Matt.' It was just a single word but it conveyed all the caring anyone could need. 'Are you OK?'

He tried to force a smile but his lips wouldn't cooperate. He shrugged an eyebrow instead. 'I'm glad it's over,' he said.

Polly nodded, her face betraying her own relief. 'Are you busy later?'

Matt looked away, his eyes scanning faces in the crowd without focussing. 'I've got a lot to catch up on.'

'Can we meet somewhere?' Polly could feel the barrier. She was still being excluded for some reason. 'I'd really like to talk to you, Matt.'

'I'm not very good company at the moment.'

Matt's statement was an excuse Polly wasn't prepared to accept. 'I'm not looking for a fun night out,' she told him gently. 'I just want to spend some time with you.'

Matt was still gazing blankly around. Looking anywhere but directly at Polly. Polly's frustration bit through her sadness.

'I loved Bonnie, too, you know.' She hadn't intended it to sound like an accusation but the brief glance she won from Matt suggested that her tone was inappropriate.

'I know.' He sounded cool. 'Thanks for everything you did for Bonnie, Polly. It meant a great deal to Russell and Karen.'

What about you? Polly wanted to ask. Did it not mean anything to you? The inability to connect gave her a fresh wave of grief. Tears gathered. 'I never even had the chance to say goodbye.'

Matt could see the moisture blurring the clarity of those dark blue eyes. The urge to hold and comfort Polly was so strong his hands began to move of their own accord. Touching her would be his undoing and Matt was grateful for the appearance of another person. Stephanie eyed Polly sympathetically and then put her arm around her friend's shoulders before glancing at Matt.

'It's all so terribly sad, isn't it?' she offered.

Matt's nod was brisk. Polly reached for a soggy handkerchief. Stephanie looked across the foyer towards where the Weavers were still fielding condolences from the numerous hospital personnel who had known their daughter.

'I wonder if it makes it any easier for Karen that they have another baby on the way?'

'Of course it doesn't.' Matt gave Stephanie a dismissive stare. 'You can't just replace one child with another.'

'I didn't mean…' Stephanie was clearly taken aback. 'I meant that it might help to have a reason to go on. Otherwise this might feel like the end of the world.'

Matt was still staring at Stephanie. 'I'm sure it does.'

Polly nodded agreement. 'The new baby could never be a replacement,' she added quietly, 'but I'm sure you're right, Steph. Even if Karen and Russell aren't aware of it just yet. They'll have a new focus and a new life.' Polly could feel her thoughts turning inwards again, drawing her own comfort from another new life. 'They'll still be a family,' she finished.

Matt was staring at Polly now. 'That wasn't what I meant.' His correction sounded offhand. 'What *I'm* sure of is that it feels precisely like the end of the world. Excuse me.'

Stephanie whistled under her breath as the two nurses watched Matt walk away. 'He's not very happy, is he?'

'No.' There were so few people here who could understand just how devastating this occasion was for Matt. Polly wanted to run after him. To take him by the hand and pull him to a place they could be alone together. Of course he didn't want to show his true feelings in public but he had to let go some time. Somewhere. What better place than with her understanding and comfort to offer support? Was it possible he had no idea of the love she had available for him? The love she so badly wanted to give?

Matt walked through the crowd and kept walking. Karen and Russell would understand when he didn't turn up at the graveside ceremony. He had to get away from everybody. He had come so close to cracking when he'd seen Polly crying. So close to allowing a connection that could have been fatal.

It wasn't just that Polly was inextricably linked to Bonnie in his mind that made it so imperative to escape. Polly carried the danger of seeming almost worth the risk of loving, despite just how big a risk Matt now knew it could be. He had to get away. He had to clear his head so that he could remind himself that no one was worth that kind of risk. Self-preservation was the key here.

Survival.

If only there was a way he could just keep on walking until he found a completely new life. Matt's stride ate up the distance between the church and his car. It wasn't until he got in and slammed the door shut that he felt the first ray of hope. Maybe there was a way he could do just that.

Escape.

CHAPTER SIX

'I'M BLAMING you.' The statement was firm.

'Oh, come on.' Stephanie was grinning as she set two steaming mugs down on the staffroom table. 'It's not that bad.'

'Yes, it is,' Polly sighed. 'I should never have let you talk me into leaving Emergency. Paediatrics is not for me.'

'You love the kids. And they love you. We all have bad days.'

Polly was silent for a moment. She wasn't just having a bad day. She was having a bad week. Probably the worst week of her entire life. Every day since the funeral had become a little worse. Contact with Matt had been frustrating. He was friendly enough but so distant. Focussed on his work. There were always excuses—albeit very good excuses—why they couldn't spend time together.

'I'm on call. There's a splenectomy case in Ward 14 that's not doing well. We might have to have another look.'

'I've simply got to get on with the mountain of paperwork on my desk. I had a complaint from a GP yesterday that a patient has been sent home and he still has no official diagnosis from the exploratory surgery.'

'Sorry, Polly, but I'm just too tired. I was up all night with one emergency after another.'

Yesterday had been a day off for Matt but when

Polly tried to ring him at home all she got was his answering machine. If he had answered there would have been another excuse. A work-related one that Polly couldn't try and argue about. He was using his job as a shield. A very effective one.

'I must admit,' Stephanie conceded, 'that kid in bed seven is the short straw for the day.'

'He's awful,' Polly agreed. 'And his mother can't cope. She wants me to give him a sedative to shut him up.'

'Did you explain that doping a three-year-old would not help the neurological checks after a skull fracture?'

'At least he's stopped vomiting. He might be able to go home soon. His mother's stressed about the older children she's left with her husband. Apparently he doesn't appreciate being left with child-care duties.'

'She's got older kids? She doesn't look old enough to have the three-year-old.'

'She's twenty-three,' Polly told her friend. 'She has a five, four and three-year-old. All boys. And she had a termination last year.'

'Good grief. Hasn't she heard of contraception?'

'It failed. The first time was when she was sixteen. She left school and married the father as the only way out. The next two pregnancies were planned—sort of. She thought it might help the marriage and that if she was home with one she might as well have a whole family. Then she went off the Pill because of the scare about blood clots and, bingo, condoms failed again.'

'Sounds careless to me.'

'It happens.' Polly's statement carried far more personal conviction than Stephanie was aware of. 'It's bad luck as much as anything. And she's paid for it. I don't think things are too happy at home.'

'I'm not surprised.' Stephanie dipped her biscuit into her mug of tea and ate it with obvious relish. 'Two mistakes don't cancel each other out.'

'Two mistakes?'

'Getting pregnant was one. Using that as a reason to get married was the second. And she's had another two kids!' Stephanie shook her head disbelievingly. 'How could she possibly have thought that would improve a marriage that shouldn't have happened in the first place?'

Polly gave no answer to the rhetorical question. *She* was pregnant. It might have been accidental but she was too much in love with Matt to consider it a mistake. It would not be the reason she would want to marry Matt but she had to concede that he might see the situation very differently.

'You know an awful lot about the family,' Stephanie commented. 'He's only been in here for a couple of hours.'

'His mum wants to talk.' Polly sighed. 'Maybe that's what I don't like about Paeds. You get far more involved with your patients.'

'But that's good,' Stephanie disagreed. 'I'd hate being in ED and shooing them out the door as fast as they came in.'

'It's got a big downside,' Polly reminded her. 'I've got to take Katy McInroe down to Theatre in a few minutes. Her parents are both in the relatives' room at the moment, sobbing in each other's arms.'

'Oh...' Stephanie's face creased sympathetically. 'That is a tough one.'

Polly nodded as she picked up her empty mug. 'I'd better go and spend some time with them.'

She walked away from the staffroom with a heavy heart. Katy was a delightful three-year-old who had come in with a fractured femur which had been the result of nothing more than a simple fall at home. The kind of stumble a toddler could make a dozen times a day and come to no harm. The X-ray in Emergency had revealed the cause of the fragile bone segment. Katy had a malignant tumour that was too large for the limb-saving surgery that would have made her treatment easier for everyone. Although the prognosis was still good, her parents were trying to cope with the knowledge that their daughter would return from Theatre later that afternoon with one leg amputated well above the knee.

Katy would cope much better than her parents. She had the kind of resilience a lot of children displayed. An ability to bounce back and get on with the business of getting the most out of life. Some children were able to do it repeatedly. Like Bonnie had.

Polly sighed deeply. Thoughts of Bonnie were never far away. Especially here at work. And thoughts of Bonnie automatically led to thoughts of Matt. She was seriously worried about him. He was too calm, too cheerful. Matt had put himself into a space enclosed by a wall of denial and Polly was not allowed to enter that space. Maybe it was time to force an entry. If Matt continued to avoid the issue he would never be able to move on, and that could be disastrous for Polly but even worse for Matt himself. If only he would call. Or turn up to see a patient.

Her gaze swept the corridor hopefully as far as the main doors, as it had so many times already that week, but the people entering the ward were not staff members. A man with two small boys came towards Polly. His expression was belligerent.

'Where's my wife?' he demanded. 'Lisa Copland.'

'Room seven,' Polly responded. 'Are you Mr Copland?'

'Yeah. Where's room seven, then?'

'I'll show you.' Polly turned, still absorbing her impression of the trio. She did not warm to Lisa's husband. Dressed in a battered denim jacket, jeans and heavy work boots, his manner was aggressive enough to be intimidating. The closely cropped hair-style with a tuft at the back left to grow into a long ponytail was mirrored by both children who scuffed their feet and followed Polly reluctantly. They did not want to be here. Lisa appeared equally reluctant to have them there.

'You'd better behave yourselves,' she warned her older sons. 'Ricky is sick.' She turned to her husband. 'Why isn't Aaron at school?'

'He said he didn't want to go. When are you coming home?'

'I don't know,' Lisa snapped defensively. 'The doctor wants Ricky watched. He's got a cracked skull.'

'I'm going to work. You'll have to come home and look after these two.'

'I can't!' Lisa's voice rose angrily. 'You'll have to stay off work, Brendon.'

'And who's going to pay the bloody bills, then?'

The older boys took advantage of their parents' confrontation to start pushing each other. Ricky shook the bars of his cot and shrieked. Polly registered the rapidly deteriorating situation with alarm. When the charge nurse entered the room at speed, Polly had never been more pleased to see the grim expression Lee was capable of projecting.

'What on earth is going on?' Lee snapped. 'Keep your voices down. You two!' Lee glared at the fighting boys. 'Cut that out. Right *now*!'

The boys stopped fighting and Lee gave a satisfied nod. She turned to deal with their father but paused fractionally. 'There's a phone call waiting in the office for you, Polly. I'll sort this out.'

Polly escaped gratefully and moved swiftly. Maybe this was the call from Matt that she had been hoping for. Her hand was trembling slightly as she picked up the receiver.

'Polly Martin speaking.'

'Hi, Polly. It's Karen.'

The surprise outweighed the disappointment that it wasn't Matt. Surprise that was quickly followed by a hefty pang of remorse.

'Karen, how *are* you?' Polly cringed inwardly at automatically asking such a stupid question. 'I'm so sorry I haven't been in touch since…since…' How could she phrase it? The death of your daughter? The funeral?

'That's OK.' Karen seemed to understand the difficulty. 'And to tell you the truth, we had too many people around to start with. It's only been in the last day or two that we've had any time to ourselves.' Karen paused and Polly sensed that whatever had prompted the call was not easy to articulate.

'Is there anything I can do to help at the moment?'

'Actually, there is,' Karen said gratefully. 'I've been having a bit of a tidy up today and when I was packing some of Bonnie's toys I had the idea of donating them to the children's ward. She spent a lot of time there over the last few years and we'd like to think that we could put something back on her behalf.'

'That's a lovely idea,' Polly said. 'But there's no rush.'

'I want to do it now,' Karen told her. 'And so does Russell.' She hesitated. 'The thing is that while we're keen to make the donation I'm not sure that we could handle visiting the ward again just yet. I wondered if you could come and collect the toys?'

'Of course.'

'Today?' Karen sounded hopeful.

'I'll come after work,' Polly promised. 'Would 4 p.m. be all right?'

Karen had a pot of coffee ready to plunge when Polly arrived. They sat in the kitchen and Polly found herself staring at the noticeboard on the wall behind the table. Pictures, obviously drawn by Bonnie, were pinned up along with dozens of photographs. Photographs from Tiger Island had pride of place but many older shots were also on display. Pictures of Karen and Russell with their daughter that fairly glowed with the obvious bond between the couple as well as with their child. The much younger Bonnie had hair that was thick and dark and wavy enough to remind Polly strongly of Matt.

'We're going to have them all made into a collage.' Karen had noticed the direction of Polly's gaze. 'And then frame it to go on a wall. That way we'll remember the good things every day. The memories won't get buried in a photo album and just dusted off occasionally.'

'I really admire the way you're coping,' Polly told her quietly. 'I can only guess at how devastating this has been for you.'

'I've got Russell,' Karen said simply. 'We keep each other strong. And when we can't then we cry together.'

'You're very lucky.' Polly was astonished to find she was envious. 'You both are—to have a relationship like that.' If only she and Matt could be like that. She had not been allowed the opportunity to offer strength or share the sadness.

Karen was watching Polly carefully. 'You loved Bonnie, too,' she said softly. The touch on Polly's hand brought tears to her eyes. The recognition of her own grief was as welcome as it was surprising. 'I'm just sorry you didn't see her in the last few days,' Karen continued. 'Or when we brought her home again.'

'I wasn't feeling well. I had to stay away from the unit.'

'I know. Matt told us.'

'And Matt said you needed time to yourselves at home. I didn't want to intrude.'

'Oh, Polly. You wouldn't have been intruding.' Karen's glance was direct. 'One of the things about Bonnie's life that we're very grateful for is the way her illness brought new people into our lives. Special people. Like Matt. And you. I'd like us to stay friends, Polly. Don't stay away. Please?'

'I won't,' Polly promised.

Karen sighed. 'Matt told us you didn't come because you were finding it too much to handle. I can't believe he let you think that you wouldn't have been welcome. I suspect he was the one having the trouble coping. He didn't even come to the graveside ceremony and we've barely seen him since.'

'I've hardly seen him at work.' Polly knew she sounded anxious. 'He's shut me out completely.'

'He's shut all of us out,' Karen said sadly. 'He thinks he's helping by being so strong and in control. I was hoping that he'd been able to talk to you if no one else.'

Polly shook her head. 'He's avoiding me.'

'He was here for dinner last night,' Karen told her. 'It was the first time since the funeral. Russ and I asked if he would consider being a godfather to our new baby. Looking forward to this baby is about the only thing keeping us going right now. There's only ten weeks or so to go now and Russ and I thought it might help Matt if he was more involved.'

'How did he react?' Polly discovered she felt nervous. She was going to have to tell Matt very soon about his own baby.

'Not well,' Karen admitted. 'In fact, he refused.'

'Why?' Nervousness blossomed into a nameless fear.

'He said that his experience of being any kind of a parent has taught him that the cost is too high. He's never going to have that kind of involvement with a child ever again. His own or anyone else's.'

Polly could feel the colour draining from her cheeks. Any nebulous thought of confiding the news of her pregnancy to Karen and asking for advice on breaking the news vanished. Approaching Matt was going to be a much tougher call now. Maybe an impossible one. It would be inviting a rejection Polly wasn't sure she would be able to face. Karen was looking at her with some concern.

'I'm sorry, Polly. I really thought that you and Matt were…that you had…' Karen paused, unsure of her territory.

'We were,' Polly confirmed. 'It started just after we came back from taking Bonnie to Australia.' She paused only fractionally. It had started then sure enough. She must have become pregnant some time during their first week together. 'I thought we had something pretty special,' she added. 'Now I'm not sure at all.'

'Has he told you about his plans to go to the UK?'

'No.' A wave of despair swept over Polly. Her next words came out as a whisper. 'When's he planning to go?'

'Next week.' Karen looked upset at being the one to break news that was clearly a shock. 'I'm amazed he hasn't said anything. It's not like him to let people down like this. I'm worried about him.'

'I'm going to talk to him,' Polly decided aloud. 'I'll take this box of toys into work and I'll go and find Matt. There's something else I need to talk to him about anyway.' She finished her coffee. The mug shook and nearly tipped as she put it down on the table. 'This time he's going to talk to me.' Polly stood up and ignored the betrayal of wobbly knees. 'I'll stay as long as it takes to make sure he does.'

'Good for you,' Karen encouraged. 'And good luck.'

A good measure of courage might be needed along with the luck. Polly had been sitting in Matt's office for twenty minutes now. She had just finished another mug of coffee and she had heard all about Matt's planned international trip.

'We've been loosely collaborating with this team in Glasgow for a few years now. They've done some very interesting work in emergency laparotomy. Particularly abdominal surgery following trauma.'

Polly had only half listened to the details about the proposed research projects that focussed on different kinds of volume replacement fluids and presurgical imaging techniques. Matt was taking refuge in sharing an enthusiasm that was strictly professional and Polly just nodded occasionally.

It was hard enough, trying to deal with the fact that Matt was going away. That he hadn't told her he was leaving. That he hadn't even seemed apologetic on confirming Karen's information. And that confronting him with the news of her pregnancy would be the worst possible approach to try and prevent his departure.

Matt was watching her now. Gauging her reaction. Polly dropped her gaze. She couldn't afford to show her true feelings. If Matt was trying to shield himself with this professionalism then her need to connect at the kind of personal level she craved would only increase his defences.

'It's only for a few weeks.' Matt made the move to more personal territory unaided. 'A month at the most. I've been meaning to take this trip for a long time and this seems like an ideal opportunity.'

Polly glanced up at the slight hesitation she detected and her gaze locked with Matt's.

'I'm not running out on you, Polly. I was going to tell you all about it as soon as I had finalised my plans.' His expression held a mute appeal that Polly couldn't help responding to. 'I need a break, Polly. This is a lot tougher than I thought it would be.'

'I know,' Polly told him gently. 'But I want to help, Matt. Don't shut me out.'

'I'm not.'

'Of course you are. I've hardly seen you for two weeks and when I do you might as well be on another planet.' Polly took a deep breath. 'I get the impression that I'm not welcome in your life any more, Matt.' Polly's voice caught painfully. 'That you buried our relationship along with Bonnie.' Polly fought the tears she could feel gathering. She stared at her hands, unable to look directly at Matt. 'Was that all it was to you, Matt? A distraction from your daughter's illness?'

'You know it wasn't. Isn't,' Matt corrected himself quickly.

Polly raised her gaze and was startled by the pain she could see in Matt's eyes. Surely a pain that deep couldn't be there unless he cared as much as she did.

'I need some time, Polly,' Matt said softly. 'I don't know where I am just now. Please, try and understand.'

Reaching out, Matt took hold of Polly's hand. The strength of his grip was startling. Polly's tears could no longer be checked. One escaped and trickled slowly down the side of her nose as she felt the connection—both physical and emotional. The strength of her love for this man was both her support and her undoing. Of course she understood. Was Matt just too afraid to admit to the kind of vulnerability that giving and receiving their kind of love brought with it? Or was denial a means of self-protection as he came to terms with the devastating loss he had just suffered?

The tears trickled faster as Polly realised there was no way she could tell Matt she was pregnant. Not yet.

The knowledge would be a trap there could be no escape from. By offering a kind of replacement, she would be taking away his opportunity to let Bonnie go. Matt needed the chance to accept both the joy and the pain Bonnie had brought to his life and then move on.

If he decided to stay, Polly would never know whether it was for her sake or the baby's. Even worse, he might ask her to consider a termination and that would be something she could never forgive. He was only going to be away for a few weeks. Long enough for her to get safely through her first trimester. Long enough for Matt to come to terms with Bonnie's death maybe. Long enough for Matt to discover that he missed her. To recognise that what they had together was special enough to build their futures around.

'Will you stay in touch?'

'Of course.' Matt squeezed her hand. 'We've got email and the phone. You probably won't even notice I'm not around.'

Polly noticed all right.

She noticed every visit of a consultant to the ward that wasn't Matt. She noticed every child that reminded her in some way of Bonnie and she noticed every night that she spent alone in her bed. How could she avoid it when she had the reminder of their love-making and how she felt about Matt with her every second of every day? The morning sickness had passed mercifully swiftly but there were other changes going on in her body. Her breasts felt full and her waistline thickened gradually, although even another month didn't make it obvious under the loose tunic and trousers of her uniform. The scan she had the week after Matt left made the reality overwhelming. The emotional reaction to seeing a tiny new heart beating within her own body had already bonded Polly to her child. Matt's child.

Communication with Matt proved surprisingly difficult. Polly's personal life was full of decisions that needed thought. The lease on her flat had expired and Polly was just renting on a weekly basis until she could decide what to do. It wasn't a suitable place for a baby and there was no way she could move herself into Helen's boisterous household in her condition. Finances on a nurse's salary had always been tight. Renting the kind of place she would like for her child was out of reach and raising a deposit to purchase even the most basic house was an impossible dream. It would have helped to talk about it, but Polly's integrity made it unacceptable to tell anybody about her pregnancy until Matt knew. She was grateful she hadn't given in to the impulse to confide in Karen, but the tone of her correspondence with Matt put paid to any notion of breaking the news to him via email.

Polly's social life was non-existent thanks to the physical weariness that overtook her each evening. That only left work to tell Matt about and sharing the stories of sick children did not seem a seem a sensitive thing to do at a time when Matt was trying to come to terms with his own child's death. She did tell him about Katy McInroe, however, and how extraordinarily well the small girl had coped with the amputation of her leg. An artificial one had been made and Katy's acceptance of the situation had inspired her parents to cope. At the suggestion of a counsellor, Katy had named her new leg and while her choice of 'Kirsty' after one of the nursing staff had led to some embarrassment, the whole family was now looking forward to Katy's readmission when her stump was healed enough for her to start learning to walk again.

All in all, communication was unsatisfactory and Polly was dismayed to find the distance between herself and Matt steadily increasing. Her nervousness about seeing Matt again also increased steadily over the course of the month. She hoped fervently that they would be able to have some private time together. How to handle a reunion at work was too awkward to even imagine.

Matt could see it was Polly even from this distance. He could hear her laugh cutting through all the sounds the busy corridor was generating between them. She must be returning from the cafeteria after a late lunch. Her friend Stephanie was beside her and they were laughing. He couldn't stop and turn. Matt was being carried along with the human traffic, getting inexorably closer to Polly with every step.

She looked far more gorgeous than he had remembered. The shine on her golden hair was echoed in a bloom on her skin. Had she put on weight while he'd been away? If she had, it suited her. The tunic top of her uniform was stretched just a little more tightly across her breasts. Matt registered the unmistakable pull of desire with dismay. If he only had to look at Polly from a distance to feel his resolve being undermined then he had more of a problem than he'd anticipated.

The resolve had formed gradually over the last month but it had firmed up considerably in the last few days. The twenty-four-hour journey back from

Scotland had been the ideal opportunity to finalise and accept his resolution. Matt had missed Polly far more than he had expected to start with. He had missed seeing her in the strange wards he had visited. And he had missed her every night as he had lain alone in his bed. He had also missed Bonnie. The sleepless hours had given him plenty of time to think and Matt believed he had come to terms with Bonnie's death. He could remember the good things without the accompaniment of unbearable grief and he could value the experience as something he wouldn't have wanted to miss.

Not that he would do it again, however, and if he allowed his relationship with Polly to be rekindled then it would inevitably lead to marriage—and children and a whole new raft of responsibility and vulnerability. He didn't want that. His time away had proved he could survive without Polly Martin in his life. It would even get easier as time went on. His time away had also given him a new interest in his career. A focus that didn't have the potential to shatter his life if it didn't go according to plan. Research was the key. And travel. A new direction. Matt's head felt really clear for the first time in months and he had arrived home with the determination to tidy up the other remnants of his previous personal life. It was only fair to Polly to let her know as soon as possible that there was no hope of any future together. She would thank him for this one day. He would never be able to offer her the kind of love she deserved, a love that would hold a whole family together. Polly would be such a wonderful mother. By ending this now, Matt would be giving Polly the chance to have the family he could never be a part of.

But it was going to be harder than he had envisaged, thanks to the betrayal by his body. His physical reaction to Polly seemed to create a force that sped across the remaining distance between them in the corridor. Polly looked up as though startled and her gaze locked with Matt's. The wide smile on her face faded and there was a moment of absolute stillness on her features. Then a new expression conveyed her joy at seeing Matt and his dismay became despair. He could never hold out against the hope and the love he saw in Polly's eyes. It reminded him so much of the way Bonnie had looked when she had been holding that tiger cub.

The memory was enough to bring Matt to his senses. This had to stop. Now. He couldn't afford to allow anybody that close again. Not now.

Not ever.

Polly was close enough now to see the subtle change in Matt's expression. The moment the shutters came down. He had been pleased to see her. More than pleased. It had been a strong enough emotional reaction for Polly to be able to sense his presence even with no warning of a possible meeting. She had had no idea he was back in the country yet let alone at work, but she had felt the connection as surely as a physical touch.

So this was it. An unexpected reunion in the place she had least wanted it. A reunion that was likely to determine her future. Polly had been waiting weeks for this; long, lonely weeks during which fear had wrestled with hope against the background of a love for Matt that she knew could never die. Polly realised that Stephanie sensed something unusual going on as well. As Polly's progress slowed, Stephanie stared at the man approaching them. Then she cast Polly a rather speculative glance.

'I'll see you back on the ward, then?'

Polly nodded. She gave up any pretence of walking.

'Matt!' Polly was careful not to let her smile and tone appear anything more than a greeting for a colleague. 'How are you?'

'Very well, thanks, Polly. And you?' Matt's glance followed Stephanie's retreating figure as he also paused. 'You're looking well.'

'I'm fine,' Polly told him. 'When did you get back?'

'Last night. It was way too late to ring anybody.'

Had he wanted to ring? Polly searched his face, looking for clues. They were almost alone in their stretch of the corridor for the moment. A bed was being pushed towards them. A dinner trolley was ahead. A family group with a child in a wheelchair skirted the obstacle they made.

'I've missed you, Matt,' Polly said quietly. 'Have you got time for a coffee?'

'Not really.' Matt was avoiding her eyes. 'There's an unbelievable mountain of mail on my desk.'

'Later, then?' Polly felt like she was knocking on a closed door but she couldn't turn away. Matt had had his time and space. She had to find out whether that door was locked.

Matt met her gaze then. Polly saw in his eyes a flash of something like...what was it? Pain? Regret? Shame? Whatever it was, it was gone as instantly as it had appeared. Suddenly she felt like she was staring at someone she didn't know at all. A complete stranger.

'I don't think so, Polly.' Matt held her gaze unblinkingly. 'I'm sorry.'

Polly gave her head a tiny shake as though trying to make sense of what she'd heard.

'Is that it, Matt?' Her voice sounded strange. The words were being forced out of a painfully constricted throat. 'Are you saying it's all over?'

'Let's be honest, Polly.' Matt looked away and nodded at the pair of consultants who were walking briskly past. He turned back as soon as they were out of earshot. 'It was a shared concern for Bonnie that brought us together. That's gone now. It has to be over.'

Polly didn't care who might be walking past. She caught Matt's arm. 'Is that all we had, Matt? Do you really believe that?'

Matt glanced down at her arm. His smile held definite regret this time. 'The sex was great,' he admitted, 'but that's not really enough, is it?'

Polly was speechless. She snatched her hand away. He was dismissing everything they'd had. Reducing it to a sordid affair based on nothing more than mutual physical pleasure. He knew as well as she did how much deeper than physical their connection had been. He knew that Polly loved him. Now he was taking her gift of love and throwing it back in her face. This was far more devastating than Polly had expected it could be. The pain was so great that Polly had to defend herself. She allowed the glow of outrage to fan itself into a flame.

'So that's it?'

Matt looked uncomfortable and Polly's breath was

expelled in a huff that was halfway between a laugh and a sob. He would look a lot more than uncomfortable if she chose this moment to inform him of his impending fatherhood.

Should she tell him?

Of course she should. He had the right to know.

'I'd better go, Polly. I've got a lot of work to get on with.'

The anger blossomed into fury. How dared he do this her? To himself? He was taking away her future. Destroying her dreams. He was denying himself the same future. Throwing away his chance of a real family. And he hadn't even had the consideration to choose a place that wasn't public. Polly had to move as a bed attended by a large medical team went by. The space created prompted Matt to follow in their wake.

'Matt.' Polly's tone was forceful enough to make him pause and turn again, an eyebrow lifted in a resigned acquiescence to hear whatever parting shot she felt obliged to deliver. Polly could feel her heart thumping. She opened her mouth to tell him and then closed it again.

Matt didn't deserve to know about the baby. He had just dumped her. She was facing a future alone and if the father of her baby didn't want her then she was damned if she was going to let him try and influence the big decisions she was facing. He would probably offer some sort of financial assistance. It was bad enough that he'd said the sex had been the only good thing about their relationship. If he offered to pay for it, the humiliation would be catastrophic. Polly could face this alone if she had to. She wanted to face it alone. Nothing this man could offer her right now would be good enough.

Matt was still waiting for her to speak. Suddenly, there was nothing that Polly wanted to say. She shook her head dismissively, turned on her heel and began walking away.

As far as she was concerned, Matthew Saunders could go to hell.

CHAPTER SEVEN

IT WAS only a matter of time before someone noticed.

The automatic stretch Polly indulged in as she rubbed the small of her back made Stephanie's eyes widen dramatically.

'My God, Polly—you're *pregnant,* aren't you?'

Polly gave the door of the drugs room a panicked glance. The reassurance that Stephanie's observation had not been overheard gave little relief. Her secret was no longer safe.

'I had my suspicions,' Stephanie told her more quietly. 'Then you came back from leave and more than one person commented that you'd put on weight. Why on earth didn't you tell me?'

'I couldn't.' Polly fiddled with the premixed insulin syringe she had come in to collect.

'Why not? I thought we were friends, Polly. Real friends.'

'We are.' Polly dropped the syringe into the blue plastic kidney dish and gave Stephanie's arm a quick squeeze. 'I'm sorry, Steph. I had to get my head around a lot of stuff and I just wasn't ready to tell anybody.'

'You mean I'm the only one who knows?'

'Apart from my mother, and I only told her last week. Promise you won't say anything. Please!' Polly reached for an alcohol wipe and added it to the kidney dish. 'I'm getting a larger size uniform today. That should keep things hidden for a few more weeks.'

'How far along are you?'

'Nearly five months.'

Stephanie emitted an awestruck whistle. 'Who's the father?'

Polly appeared to be concentrating on calibrating the blood-glucose monitor she had taken from the shelf. She avoided her friend's curious stare. 'I'd rather not say.'

'Fair enough.' Stephanie checked the drug chart on the bench in front of her and reached for a bottle of tablets on the top shelf. 'I think I know who it is, anyway.' She lowered her voice again. 'It's Matt Saunders, isn't it?'

Polly knew she was probably failing to look as though Stephanie couldn't be further from the truth and her query came out sounding distinctly lame. 'What makes you think that?'

Stephanie's smile conceded that it had been a valiant effort. 'Come on, Polly. I saw the way you looked at him—that day we were coming back from lunch and you spotted him in the corridor. I had a chance to think on my way back to the ward. You'd been miserable ever since Bonnie's funeral. For as long as Matt Saunders had been out of the country. Then you suddenly took two weeks' leave after he got back.' Her gaze was sympathetic now. 'I take it he's not too keen on the idea of fatherhood?'

'He doesn't know I'm pregnant.'

'What?' Stephanie's jaw dropped. The bottle of tablets in her hand tipped and filled the tiny plastic cup. Polly smiled.

'I don't fancy your chances getting Reece Jenson to swallow that lot. I had enough trouble getting one pill into him yesterday. Mind you...' Polly eyed the large tablets '...they are the size of small footballs.'

'He's nine,' Stephanie said firmly. 'He was told what the consequences would be if he continued spitting out the syrup. It was his choice to take the tablets rather than have injections. Anyway...' Stephanie was putting the extra tablets back into the bottle '...don't change the subject. Why on earth haven't you told him?'

The arrival of another nurse made the tiny room very crowded. It also prevented Polly answering the difficult question.

'Melanie's due for her blood-glucose measurement and insulin shot.' Polly picked up the kidney dish. 'She's going to try and do it herself this morning, which is a bit of a breakthrough. I'll talk to you later, Steph.'

'You sure will,' Stephanie said darkly. 'We've got some catching up to do.'

The feeling of relief as Polly hurried to attend to a busy day's duties wasn't due simply to her reprieve. She was relieved that Stephanie had guessed. She was even more relieved that her friend hadn't taken more offence at having been excluded from the momentous developments in her life. Polly now had a chance to discuss her situation with someone who might offer more positive advice than her mother had been able to. The prospect was cheering and Polly found herself really enjoying her work for the first time in weeks.

Ten-year-old Melanie Smith coped with a self-administered finger prick test to check her blood-sugar levels, read the monitor score and recorded it in her diary. She screwed up her courage even further to give the subcutaneous injection of insulin into a fold of skin on her abdomen.

'Well done, chicken.' Polly gave her a hug. 'I'm proud of you.'

'It didn't really hurt that much,' Melanie confessed. 'It's the thinking about doing it that's worse.'

'That's often the case,' Polly agreed. Maybe the apprehension would also be worse than the event when she finally steeled herself to break the news to Matt as she knew she would eventually have to. Practising on Stephanie would be very helpful. She smiled at Melanie.

'As soon as Mum gets here I'm going to take you both down to visit the dietician. She's going to talk to you about how important your diet is going to be.'

'Does that mean I'm fat?'

'No.' Polly chuckled. 'You're as skinny as a rake. When you have diabetes it means that your body has trouble adjusting the levels of sugar in your blood. The medicine you're learning to take means that you have to be careful about what you eat and when you eat it. She'll explain it all to you.'

'Are you coming with us?'

'Only to show you where to go. I've got lots of other patients to look after today and there's a new boy coming in soon. I need to get his bed made.'

'What's wrong with him?'

'I believe he's got a broken arm that's bad enough to need an operation.'

Polly passed a physiotherapist encouraging her young patient to walk on her crutches.

'Hello, Katy!' Polly crouched, a wide smile lighting her features. 'Look at you!'

'I'm taking Kirsty for a walk.' Katy was concentrating hard. 'Watch.'

Polly was only too happy to watch. Katy was having trouble getting Kirsty the leg to co-operate and her mother hovered anxiously on one side, ready to catch her.

'I'm tired, Mummy.'

The physiotherapist shook her head fractionally. 'One more step, sweetheart. Kirsty goes with the crutches and then you move your other leg.'

The effort was rewarded by a cuddle in her mother's arms. The physio picked up the tiny crutches. 'How 'bout we go for a swim in the hot pool?'

'Does Kirsty come, too?'

'Of course. She'll have to sit and watch while you swim, though.'

Polly moved on. She had a room to set up for the new arrival. Surgery was apparently scheduled for later that afternoon, which didn't allow much time to settle and reassure a newcomer. She could only afford a few seconds' pause when Stephanie caught up with her in the corridor.

'What are you doing after work?'

'Going home to blob out on the couch, I expect.' Polly grinned. 'I've had it by the time I've been on my feet all day.'

'Wrong answer.' Stephanie shook her head. 'Well, you can blob out if you want to, but I'll be sitting on the other end of the couch. I'll pick up some takeaways and be at your flat by six-thirty. Unless you'd rather go out somewhere?'

'No. Come round to my place. I really am tired these days. And ravenous.' Polly eyed the sandwiches

Stephanie was carrying. She was looking forward to her own lunch-break.

'I'll bring extra take-aways,' Stephanie promised. 'Chinese food OK?'

'Sounds great.'

'I don't think I can fit in even one more noodle.' Polly eyed the containers littering her table. 'You brought enough food to feed an army.'

'You've eaten enough to feed an army.' Stephanie reached for the wine bottle to refill her glass. 'Shame you can't have any of this. It's a great Chardonnay.' She closed her eyes to savour the mouthful she took. Then her eyes snapped open. 'OK,' she announced. 'I'm ready. Talk to me, Polly.'

Polly groaned. 'Where do I start?'

'Let's work backwards. Here you are more than halfway to producing a baby and the father doesn't know about it. Why the hell not?'

'He ended the relationship before I had a chance to tell him.'

Stephanie looked sceptical. 'How long does it take to say, "Hey, guess what? I'm pregnant"?'

'I was waiting for the right moment.' Polly sighed. 'OK, I was waiting for him to tell me that he loved me. If he told me that after he knew I was carrying his child, it wouldn't mean the same. I'd never know if he wanted me or the baby. I waited so long I found out he didn't want me *or* the baby.'

'How do you know he doesn't want the baby if he doesn't know about it?'

'Because I know he doesn't want children.'

'Did he *say* that?'

Polly remembered Karen's words. Matt never

wanted to be involved with a child again—his own or anybody else's. She nodded silently.

Stephanie drank more of her wine before giving Polly a quizzical glance.

'Do you love him?'

Polly nodded again.

'Really? But Matt Saunders is so... He's kind of...' Stephanie gave up on her attempt to avoid offence. 'Boring,' she concluded.

Polly had to smile. She had thought the same thing herself once. Stephanie hadn't seen Matt Saunders shinny up a tree. Hadn't heard him singing 'Puff the Magic Dragon'. Hadn't seen him holding his daughter's hand while she slept, with tears running down his face. Hadn't seen the depth of emotion those brown eyes could convey or felt the touch of his lips or hands. Hands that could... Polly collected her thoughts with difficulty.

'He's not boring,' she said quietly. 'I've been in love with him for a long time now and I know I'll never feel the same way about any other man.'

'So what went wrong?' Stephanie grinned mischievously. 'He obviously liked you enough to get you pregnant.'

'Bonnie Weaver died.'

Stephanie looked puzzled. 'What's that got to do with you and Matt Saunders?'

'Matt has been a close friend of the Weavers for years.' Polly had to choose her words carefully. Even now, she had no intention of betraying Matt's confidence. 'He was like an uncle to Bonnie and they were very close. Her death hit him very hard.'

'That just proves he loves kids. He'd feel even more strongly about one of his own.'

'That might be the problem. Maybe he doesn't want the risk of loving and losing someone else.'

'You won't know unless you tell him. You'll *have* to tell him, Polly.'

'I know. I will.'

'When?'

'Soon.'

'He won't be very happy if he hears it from someone else.'

'He won't. No one here knows except you and you've promised not to say anything, remember?'

Stephanie gave Polly a look of fond exasperation. 'Reality check, Polly Martin. There's no getting away from this. You're getting fat. Matt sees you on the ward at least a few times every week. He's not stupid.'

'I'll leave work.'

'Could you afford to?'

Polly shook her head sadly. 'No way.'

'Can your family help?'

Polly sighed heavily. 'Mum's offered to break the news to Dad and persuade him to let me live at home again, but I'd have to be desperate to consider it.'

'Is home that bad?'

Polly avoided a direct answer. 'I have every intention of coping on my own.'

'Babies are expensive.'

'I know.'

'Matt Saunders must be rich,' Stephanie said thoughtfully.

Polly thought of Matt's penthouse apartment and the elegant furnishings. 'Probably.'

'The baby is his responsibility as well, you know. He'd help. He'd have to.'

'I'm sure he would. I don't want his money, Steph. It would be like he was paying for the sex.'

'He might offer to marry you.'

'I wouldn't want that either.'

'Why not? I thought you said he was the only man you're ever going to love.'

'Remember what you said about Lisa Copland—that young mother with the three little boys? The two mistakes? Getting pregnant, and then marrying because of it?'

'This is different.'

'Why? Because he's a consultant surgeon instead of a drain layer? Because he's wealthy?'

'Because Lisa wasn't in love with the father of her baby. You are.'

'That makes it worse. He doesn't feel the same way about me.'

'He might if you gave him the chance. This baby gives you a reason to try again. If you love him that much and you have a child together, surely you can build a future on that?'

'My mother gave me one good piece of advice last week,' Polly said sombrely. 'She told me to never marry a man if he didn't love me as much as I loved him. She said it was tempting to think that you could make it happen after marriage or that having a baby would make the difference, but it can't. If the balance starts out too heavily weighted on one side, there's nothing you can do to change it and you'll break your heart trying.'

'Phew!' Stephanie shook her head. 'That's pretty heavy maternal advice.'

'I think she knows what she's talking about,' Polly said. 'My parents have a rather empty marriage. Kind of a habit that neither of them intends to break. I grew up wondering if they even liked each other that much. It's not the kind of family I'd wish on anyone, especially my own child.'

'You're right.' Stephanie drained her glass of wine. 'It was a bad idea.'

'It's a tempting idea,' Polly confessed. 'I know my mother's right but I'm still having a hard time keeping myself convinced. I can't help thinking that maybe it would be different in my case. Maybe Matt *does* love me that much but he just doesn't realise it. Or maybe he's too scared to admit it.'

'And you're too scared to tell him you're pregnant,' Stephanie reminded her. 'What happens next?'

'I don't know,' Polly admitted. 'I'm working on it. Something will happen.'

'I'm sure it will,' Stephanie agreed. 'Probably sooner than you realise.'

Stephanie Millar's estimate of the time frame for new events was quite correct. Her estimate of the number of times each week that Matt saw Polly was not but, then, she didn't know about the ways his eyes involuntarily scanned the corridors of the hospital or the tables in the cafeteria. Matt had seen Polly at least six times that week already and it was only Thursday.

The way his physical reaction to seeing Polly hadn't diminished, despite ending the relationship, was disturbing. Maybe guilt was playing a part. The suggestion that sex had been the only thing other than Bonnie holding them so closely together was as untrue as it had been hurtful, and Matt regretted the remark even though it had had the desired effect at the time. The pain and anger he had caused led to a few awkward moments as their paths crossed but Matt weathered the guilt. His head knew quite well he'd done the right thing. Perhaps a little more time was needed for his heart and body to catch up. The two weeks Polly had been away on leave recently should have helped, but strangely it had made things worse. Matt had found himself concerned by her absence, and the pleasure of spotting her again when she returned to work had been shockingly intense.

Matt was only half listening to the senior registrar beside him as they stood in the corridor of the paediatric ward. He was watching Polly, who had now made it as far as the door to the ward office only a few metres from where he stood. Her progress down the wide corridor had been very slow. Holding one of her hands was a small girl with a cloud of blonde curls and a wide smile. The child was limping badly but Matt had seen this particular child on crutches only a few days ago. Katy McInroe was making extraordinarily good progress in learning to walk with her artificial limb.

Polly was laughing now. The sound was contagious enough to make Matt smile unconsciously. Richard Parry realised that his consultant hadn't heard a word of the case of suspected appendicitis he was trying to present, so he gave up and watched Polly himself as she crouched down and swung Katy into her arms for a congratulatory hug. Katy shouted gleefully and wrapped her arms and her good leg around her nurse.

Richard's jaw drooped noticeably. Matt Saunders simply stared for a second before his gaze snapped back to his registrar.

'Where's this appendix?' he demanded. 'We haven't got all day to waste.'

Richard took one more glance over his shoulder before grabbing the case notes and trailing after the rapidly moving surgeon. The glance confirmed that he hadn't made a mistake. The small girl's leg had circled Polly's waist at a high level. The fabric of her tunic top was stretched tightly across her abdomen. There was no doubt at all that Polly Martin was pregnant.

The thirteen-year-old girl in bed two was fortunate that Richard Parry was an excellent senior registrar. The shock of seeing the unbelievable rendered Matt somewhat unprofessionally detached as he supervised Richard's examination and treatment plan. Once in the controlled familiarity of Theatre Matt regained command of his wayward thought processes, though it was Richard who performed the surgery and confirmed the diagnosis of appendicitis. By the time Matt completed his day's work by attending to paperwork in his office, the shock had worn off. Possibly driven away by the outrage that replaced it.

He couldn't be wrong. Polly had to be pregnant, and several months gone by the look of her. Matt knew with absolute certainty who the father of that baby was. It was Donna all over again. A child of his was going to come into the world without the mother having the decency to inform him of the fact. Maybe Polly was also planning to have the baby adopted and simply wipe the mistake from her life.

Matt's fist clenched around the ballpoint pen he was holding with enough force to snap the plastic barrel. The small spring bounced to the floor as he dropped the dismembered pen onto his desk. Matt stood up and moved swiftly. How the hell did Polly expect to get away with this?

She couldn't.

She wouldn't.

Not if he had anything to do with it.

The drive to Polly's flat took only minutes. Matt hadn't bothered to ring and give any advance warning of his visit. His knock on the glass pane of her door was authoritative enough to come very close to cracking the pane. The way the colour drained from Polly's face when she opened the door gave Matt a distinct flash of satisfaction. She was as aware as he was of the moral advantage he had. The look he gave Polly made no attempt to disguise his anger. He stepped past the door being held open wordlessly and didn't turn until he heard it click shut. Then he turned. Slowly. He didn't look at Polly's face. The soft T-shirt and close-fitting track pants did nothing to soften the lines of her rounded belly. His accusation was deliberately harsh.

'You had no intention of telling me, did you?'

'That's not true. I wanted to tell you. When I found out, I couldn't wait to tell you.'

Matt's snort was derisive. 'And when was that, precisely?'

'It was, precisely, when Bonnie was dying.' A small amount of colour had returned to Polly's cheeks. She straightened her back as she spoke. There was no way she could avoid this confrontation. She had done that for far too long already and Matt had every right to be angry.

'I couldn't say anything at that point.' Polly broke the stunned silence that had greeted her last response. 'And at the funeral you said you didn't think Karen's pregnancy would be helping them cope with anything. You said you couldn't replace one child with another. If I'd told you it would have seemed like I was offering *you* a replacement for Bonnie.'

Polly took a deep breath. Matt was still silent. He was still staring at her as though she had deliberately destroyed his life, but at least he appeared to be listening.

'I knew how badly Bonnie's death hit you. You wouldn't let me get close enough to even try and help. I thought I was doing the right thing in giving you the space you wanted. It would have been the worst possible time to tell you I was pregnant.'

'That was nearly *three months* ago.' Matt's emphasis was scathing.

'I saw Karen about a week after the funeral. She told me what you said when they asked you to be a godfather to the new baby. That you never wanted to be any kind of a parent to a child again. Your own or anybody else's. And then…' Polly's voice rose as she shook her head with disbelief. 'Then you ran away.'

'I didn't *run* away,' Matt contradicted coldly. 'I needed some time. A focus that wasn't so introspective. I couldn't think about anything clearly—not on a personal level. Focussing on work has helped in the past. I thought it would again.'

'And it did help, didn't it?' Polly let him see just how hurt she'd been. She held his gaze and allowed herself to relive the pain he'd caused. 'You came back knowing exactly what you wanted. Or what you didn't want, anyway. Me,' she said bitterly. 'You dumped me, Matt. Without even having the courtesy to tell me why. Would you really have expected me to think that was the right time to tell you I was having your baby?'

Matt tore his gaze away from Polly's face. His body felt heavy but he needed to move. Had he really been so unapproachable? And cruel enough to have caused the agony he'd seen in the depths of Polly's eyes? Had he really known how huge a gift of caring he had discarded? Matt knew the truth was all in affirmatives. How could he have done this to her? He had protected himself but it had been Polly who had paid the price. Matt had never considered himself to be a selfish person before. Had he really believed he had done Polly a favour by ending their relationship?

She probably hated him now. She certainly had cause to.

He walked slowly to the small couch and sat down with a heartfelt sigh.

'I'll tell you why,' he said quietly. 'I knew that if I allowed our relationship to continue it would probably lead to marriage. And children.' He gave Polly a brief glance. 'I had just lost a daughter I loved as much as if I'd been able to be her real father. I wasn't about to let that happen again. I couldn't have survived.'

It was Polly's turn to be silent. So Matt *had* been thinking about marriage. He had been trying to protect himself. Had Polly also been correct in thinking he had really loved her?

'And they say history never repeats itself,' Matt said bitterly. He rubbed a hand across his forehead. 'You know, if you'd sat down and tried to think up the worst possible thing you could have done to me, you couldn't have come up with a better plan. What was the next step, Polly? Have the baby and adopt it out so I'd never know anything about it?'

Polly was shocked. 'I'm not giving up my baby!'

'*Our* baby,' Matt snapped. He raised an eyebrow. 'Unless I'm making an incorrect assumption here? We did use contraception as I remember. Maybe that's the reason you haven't told me. Maybe I wasn't the only man you were sleeping with at the time.'

'You *bastard!*' Polly gasped. Matt's anger was hard enough to bear but at least she knew it was justified. The suggestion that her love had not been genuine and that she wasn't to be trusted hurt a lot more. Tears stung her eyes and she blinked them angrily away. She wouldn't give Matt the satisfaction of knowing how much power he still had to hurt her.

Matt was watching her closely. Silently. Polly was absolutely right. He was being and had been a bastard. And he hated himself for it. He owed her far more than any apology could account for. He could probably never make good the damage but at least he could try. He would just have to find a way to make reparation without making things worse for Polly in the long run. Helping her cope with the immediate problems her pregnancy presented would be as good a place as any to start.

Matt sighed heavily. 'All right, then. We've got some talking to do, Polly. Some decisions to make. Why don't you come and sit down?'

'I'm quite capable of managing this by myself.' Polly stayed where she was. She stood, facing Matt, her arms protectively wrapped across her belly.

'Really? And are you planning to live here?' Matt's gaze shifted and raked the tiny flat. He could see almost all of it from where he sat on the couch—the galley kitchen to one side, the single bedroom and totally inadequate bathroom.

'I'm looking for another house.'

'Have you found one yet?'

'Nothing suitable,' Polly confessed tightly. 'I'm working on it.' In actual fact, she was getting tired of spending her days off looking for new accommodation. The knowledge that anything attractive was well beyond what she could afford was becoming depressing. Frightening. She had her child's future to consider now as well as her own. The thought of someone else helping to solve the problem was appealing.

'My apartment's not really suitable either,' Matt said. 'You need a real house. With a garden. There's lots of nice places near my apartment block.'

'I couldn't afford anything in that kind of area.'

'But I could,' Matt said calmly. He seemed to make an effort to relax his expression as he held Polly's gaze. 'It's hard to talk properly with you standing there towering over me. Come and sit down... please?'

Polly complied slowly. Maybe the worst of this confrontation was over now. Maybe she could cope with the physical proximity the small couch would enforce. Matt was clearly not going to run away from his responsibilities. They needed to clarify just what sort of involvement he was going to have.

'You choose a house,' Matt told Polly. 'I'll help you pay for it.'

'I don't want your money.' Polly sat on the very edge of the couch, as far away from Matt as possible, pressed hard against the upholstered arm.

'I don't give a damn about how proud you are, Polly. We're talking about the future of my child.'

'*Our* child.'

'Exactly. And this child is going to grow up in a

decent house. She's going to have two parents and she's—'

'It's a boy.'

Matt stared, stunned into silence by the interruption. The reality hit him properly for the first time. This wasn't just Polly's pregnancy or the knowledge that in a matter of weeks a child carrying his genes would enter the world. This was a real person they were talking about. A boy. A *son*. Matt cleared his throat.

'Are you sure?'

'It was pretty obvious on the second scan.' A tiny smile played with the corner of Polly's mouth. She recognised the sense of wonder in Matt's expression. The moment when the idea of the baby had become far more personal. Real. She wished Matt had been there to see the tiny limbs moving and feel that magic moment of connection. 'He was sucking his thumb,' she added softly. 'I've got a picture if you'd like to see it.'

Matt simply nodded. The print was easy to locate, held on to the front of Polly's fridge with a frog-shaped magnet. This time, Polly sat a little closer on the couch, waiting patiently as Matt's focussed concentration absorbed the evidence of the life inside her. Matt found he was close to tears. A wave of emotion he couldn't define held him in thrall. He hadn't met Bonnie until she was two years old. He'd never felt a connection with an infant, let alone a baby that hadn't yet been born. He couldn't compare this child to Bonnie. This was a new life. A new chance.

'I want this child, Polly,' Matt said softly as he laid the photograph down.

'So do I.'

They stared at each other.

'We'll have to get married.' It was a statement rather than a question.

'Really?' Polly's tone was cool. This was as far away from her fantasy proposal from Matt as it could have been. 'Why?'

'I would have thought that was obvious.'

'Not really,' Polly said as calmly as she could. She turned her head to glance at the door. 'I don't see my father standing around with a shotgun.' Her gaze returned to the man beside her. 'It's actually no big deal to be an unmarried mother these days, Matt. Some women even choose to become one.'

'Oh?' Matt's eyes narrowed fractionally. 'And are you one of those women, Polly?'

'No.' Polly dropped her gaze quickly. 'Given the choice, I would have waited for marriage…to someone who loved me as much as I loved them. Someone who wanted a child as much as I did.'

'I do want this child,' Matt said quietly. 'OK, maybe I wouldn't have chosen to have one at this point in my life, but it's happened. I'm not going to let history repeat itself any further. I intend to be a proper father this time.' Matt took a deep breath and Polly could feel his gaze fastened on her bent head. 'I want to provide a home for my son. I want him to have my name. I want him to have both his birth parents to raise him.'

'He will have both his parents. It doesn't mean they have to be married. Or even living together.'

'It would be better if they were.'

Polly shook her head, still avoiding eye contact. 'I'm not going to marry you, Matt.'

'Why not?'

'Because you don't love me.'

Matt was silent. Polly could sense the struggle he was engaged in. Was he just trying to find the right words or had he put the shutters down so firmly on past emotions that they were impossible to locate? He *had* loved her. Polly was sure of that. The glimpses into his soul that those dark eyes had provided had made her sure, but they were buried now. Had been buried along with Bonnie. If Matt recognised that then Polly would be quite prepared to forgive his treatment of her. If he admitted his vulnerability and allowed Polly to step past the barriers he had erected, however briefly, there would be hope for a future together. Things wouldn't be the same but they could be even better. If Matt was prepared to take that risk then Polly would know just how precious a gift that trust would be.

'I...' Matt hesitated and cleared his throat, and at precisely the same moment his mobile phone began to ring. The groan Polly suppressed was forgotten when she heard Matt begin to talk.

'Calm down, Russell,' he said calmly. 'It's perfectly normal. Sometimes the waters can break a long time before the baby is born.' He listened again before clearly interrupting. 'Russell? Russell, listen. Call an ambulance or a taxi. I don't think you're in any fit state to drive Karen to the hospital. I'll ring the labour ward and let them know you're coming in. I'll meet you there.' Matt snapped his phone shut and then smiled ruefully at Polly. 'This could turn into a long night.'

'How's Karen?'

'I think she'd be a lot less nervous if Russell wasn't in a state of total panic.'

'At least you'll be able to help.'

'Are you working tomorrow?'

'No, it's a day off.'

'Good.' Matt had opened his phone again and he punched in a series of numbers. 'Labour ward, thanks,' he instructed the operator.

'Why is that good?' Polly asked during his wait.

'I want you to come, too.' Matt's glance held Polly's. 'Please,' he added softly. 'I need some help coping with this,' he confessed. 'I need you, Polly.'

The tiny crack of light between the boards of those shutters was no more than a faint gleam but it was more than enough for Polly.

'Of course I'll come, Matt.'

Sophie Anne Weaver came into the world nine hours later at 5.30 a.m. to be greeted by her parents and their support team of Matt and Polly. The long, hard labour was forgotten as Karen cradled the baby on her breasts, still sitting against Russell who had been holding his wife during the final stage. What appeared to be a telepathic message passed between Karen and Russell as they both tore their eyes from the infant to share a long glance that advertised their love and pride in each other. The picture of the new family was far too poignant for anyone who knew this couple's background and Polly made no attempt to conceal her tears. She was unaware of how close Matt was standing beside her until he touched her shoulder gently.

'Let's give them a few minutes alone,' he suggested quietly. Polly nodded, wiping her face with her fingers as she followed Matt from the room. He stopped in a deserted waiting area and turned. Polly was struck by his pale face, the lines deeply etched around his eyes, the sheer exhaustion of sharing such an emotional experience making his eyes look almost black. She probably looked just as shattered. She certainly felt it.

'Marry me, Polly,' Matt said softly. 'You have to. It's the best solution for all of us.'

Polly wanted to say yes very badly. She wanted to believe that when she held Matt's son in her arms he would look at her the way Russell had looked at Karen. But even now, when Matt's defences had to have been stripped away by the toll the long hours of last night had taken, Polly could still not feel the connection she knew she needed. Sadly she shook her head.

'No. Being pregnant is not a good enough reason to get married. It could never work.'

'We could make it work.'

'No,' Polly repeated. 'Marriage isn't something that works because people have good intentions. It's a living entity, Matt. It has good bits and bad bits. It needs commitment and determination.'

'I know that. It needs respect and affection—the establishment and maintenance of trust.' Matt's smile was tentative. 'Like training tigers.'

'It needs more than that, Matt.' Polly had to concentrate on choosing her words through the fog of her fatigue. 'Above anything else, it requires love. Enough love to provide the glue that holds it all together. A love that means being with that person is as important as the best of whatever else life has to offer and strong enough to withstand the worst of whatever life can dish out. If you don't believe you have that much love then there's no point in getting married.' Polly's sigh was almost a sound of despair. 'Great sex doesn't equal love.'

'I regret that remark.' Matt's tone was serious. 'More than I can say. We had more than that. You know we did.' He caught one of Polly's hands. 'Don't you remember what it was like when we were together? When we made love?'

Oh, God. Polly could remember it all only too well. She tried to slam the lid down on the memories. She couldn't afford to be distracted by how she had felt. How she still felt. This was about how Matt felt about her.

'You walked out on our relationship, Matt.'

'I had my reasons. Compelling reasons.'

'I accept that.' Polly nodded but her expression was sombre. 'But the fact remains that our relationship wasn't important enough. I couldn't have done that to you, Matt, and as far as I'm concerned it's proof that your feelings are nothing like mine. And never could be.'

'They might.' Matt took Polly's other hand. He held them both tightly, his eyes never leaving her face. 'Give me a chance. Give us all a chance.' His fingers moved over hers. 'At least take some time to think about my proposal.'

'Oh, I'll do that all right.' Polly's smile was wistful. 'You can count on it.'

'How much time do you need? A few days? A week? A month, maybe?'

'Give me a month,' Polly agreed. 'I think we both need some time.'

'Can we see each other? Start again, perhaps?'

Polly smiled again as she nodded. Despite her utter weariness and all the pain of the last weeks, the thought of seeing Matt again was exciting. A month was a long time. Enough time for something to change or at least to find out whether there was any hope of change.

'A month.' Matt returned her nod. 'And then, Polly Martin, I have every intention of proposing to you again.'

CHAPTER EIGHT

THE most obvious change over the next month was the shape of Polly's body.

As if to make up for being discreet for so long, her abdomen expanded rapidly enough for Polly to wonder whether the ultrasound technician had somehow missed the fact that she was carrying twins. Everybody knew about the pregnancy now. And everybody knew that Matt Saunders was the father of her child. How could they not know when Matt made a point of speaking to Polly every time he was on the ward and they were seen having lunch together in the cafeteria so often?

Gossip was rife as the hospital grapevine considered the implications of Matt's lengthy trip overseas and the fact that Polly had taken two weeks' leave so soon after his return. Only Stephanie knew the truth about how recently Matt had learned about his child, and Polly was grateful for her friend's trustworthiness. She wasn't enjoying being the subject of gossip and knew it must be much worse for Matt when he had preserved his privacy for so long. They were the subjects of many whispered conversations and curious glances. Some glances were distinctly disapproving, such as the one Polly was receiving right now from Lee Fenton.

'I must say you kept it all remarkably quiet.' Lee had waited until the other staff members had dispersed from the morning handover meeting. 'I had no idea you had a relationship with Mr Saunders.'

'Mmm.' Polly was searching for a set of patient notes amongst those littering the huge office desk. She had been assigned to special a patient she knew today. Melanie Smith had been an emergency admission during the night. Her diabetes had run out of control due to illness and she had come in to be treated for diabetic ketoacidosis. There was a slight risk that the treatment could cause cerebral oedema so she needed very careful monitoring for the next twenty-four hours.

'You should have informed me as soon as you knew you were pregnant,' Lee continued. 'What if you'd been exposed to something infectious like German measles?'

'I had my immunity checked,' Polly responded warily. Her stomach was in the way as she leaned across the desk to retrieve Melanie's file. 'I wasn't aware that I had to make my pregnancy public at that point.'

'It would have been a courtesy.'

'Yes, of course. I'm sorry I couldn't tell you.'

'I'm sure you had your reasons.' Lee now looked as curious as many people had over the last couple of weeks, but Polly simply nodded. 'I suppose you'll let me know in good time when you plan to stop working.' Lee's glance shifted to Polly's rounded stomach. 'That can't be too far away.'

'I'm only twenty-four weeks,' Polly said. 'I hope to keep working for another twelve weeks or so.' She met Lee's stern gaze. 'I don't want too much time at home to sit and worry about any birth complications or congenital problems the baby might have.'

To Polly's amazement, Lee smiled understandingly. 'You'll be fine,' she said. 'And so will the baby. We tend to get a rather prejudiced view, working in a place like this. I have five children and I worried myself sick about every one of them before they were born. They've all been very healthy. In fact…' Lee's smile broadened '…I'm expecting my first grandchild any day now.'

'Really?' Lee clearly kept her private life to herself as much as Matt had done in the past. Polly was sorry she had never seen past the strict professional façade the charge nurse used to keep her ward running so efficiently. 'Congratulations. I hope the birth goes well.'

'It will.' Lee sounded confident. 'And so will yours. You'll find the antenatal classes help. I've been going along to them with my daughter.' Lee lowered her voice. 'She doesn't have a partner who wants to be part of this.'

'Oh.' Polly wondered how Lee would react if she knew that Matt would never have chosen his own involvement with parenthood again. It would be nice to have a mother who was clearly as supportive as Lee was being for her daughter. Polly bit back the dangerous impulse to confide in the older woman. 'I start my classes next month.'

Polly left the office and tried to stop thinking about her upcoming classes. Or her pregnancy. Or Matt. She had a busy day ahead of her. Melanie had been sick with a respiratory virus for a few days before her admission. She had been taking cough medicine and sucking lozenges and her mother was unsure about how compliant she had been with the insulin injections the ten-year-old now insisted on doing privately.

She had had two days of increased hunger and thirst, had started getting up during the night to urinate and had then developed abdominal pain and headache. She had been brought into hospital after she began vomiting and became unusually lethargic. Now she was dehydrated, dangerously hyperglycaemic and her heart rhythm was affected by the chemical imbalance in her body.

'Hi, there, chicken.' Polly relieved Kirsty who had been taking the last round of observations on Melanie. 'How are you feeling?'

'Sick.' Melanie only opened her eyes briefly and Polly checked the chart Kirsty had filled in. Her patient's level of consciousness was down slightly due to her sleepiness and it would need constant monitoring. Any further deterioration could be a sign of cerebral oedema.

An initial dose of insulin had been administered, along with the fluids Melanie needed to correct her dehydration. The IV fluids were still running with a lower dose of insulin and Polly was due to add the additional medications or bicarbonate and potassium to the infusion.

'I'm going to check your blood pressure and a few other things,' she told Melanie. 'I've got a machine here to take a trace of your heart. I'll need to put some sticky patches on your chest.'

'They did that in the emergency department.' Melanie's parents were in the room with their daughter. They stood to one side of her bed at the moment, holding each other's hands. It was her father that spoke. Polly nodded.

'They may have explained to you that the trace showed some abnormalities caused by Melanie's condition. The doctor wants another trace ready to see when she comes in soon for the ward round.'

Melanie's mother was looking very anxious. 'I should have insisted on watching Melanie with her insulin. She's too young to manage by herself.'

'No, I'm not.' Melanie's eyes looked dull. Her skin was flushed and dry-looking but Polly was pleased to see her irritable but quick response.

'An illness can upset things pretty easily, even when patients are managing their injections and glucose measurements perfectly well.'

'We did forget to check more often when she got sick.'

Polly recorded the blood-pressure measurement she had taken and felt Melanie's pulse. The rate was fast and she could feel the thump of an occasional extra beat. She reached for the packet of electrodes and began positioning them to record the ECG. She noticed that Melanie's parents were still holding hands and she caught the glance that passed between the couple. The body language suggested a strong relationship and it reminded Polly of Karen and Russell. Much of the time she and Matt had spent together over the last few weeks had been in the company of the Weavers who were in a state of domestic bliss, albeit a slightly stressed bliss, since they had brought Sophie home. Their happiness had increased on learning of Polly's pregnancy. Easily persuaded that she and Matt were together again as a couple and happy to be expecting their first child, the Weavers wanted to share the joys of having a new baby at home.

Polly clipped the leads onto the electrodes. 'Keep nice and still for a bit, Melanie.' It took a few seconds for the trace to settle enough to be worth recording.

Seeing Karen and Russell together and the way Melanie's parents were drawing strength from each other only underlined what she and Matt were missing. For those couples, their children were a bonus. The relationships were quite strong enough to survive on their own. She and Matt had not had a relationship that strong. Although the last month had brought them steadily closer, again it bothered Polly a lot that it was the baby that had brought them back together. Matt hadn't wanted her purely for her own sake and that could well mean that what they had was not enough to base a marriage on. Not unless she was prepared to end up in a marriage as empty as her parents'.

'This looks a bit better.' Polly ripped off the ECG trace. The T waves were less inverted but still abnormal. It was time Polly added the medications intended to deal with the cardiac disturbance. She excused herself to collect the drugs and almost ran into Matt who was walking past Melanie's room.

'Polly!' Matt looked genuinely pleased to see her. 'How are you? Not too tired after our late night?'

'Not at all.' Polly ignored the knowing smile that Matt's senior registrar, Richard Parry, bestowed on her. She listened to Matt speaking while her thoughts ran elsewhere. Of course people would assume that she and Matt had an active sexual relationship—she was, after all, advertising the fact rather blatantly. In fact, she and Matt had not been to bed together once in the month since they had started seeing each other again. Not that it had been Polly's choice. The attraction Matt held for her had increased, if anything, during their time apart, but the fact that she was pregnant seemed to be making a huge difference. She'd been too shy to give Matt any encouragement because she was waiting for a sign that he didn't find it offputting. She'd wondered if she was simply getting fatter and less attractive by the week—or was Matt reluctant to initiate anything because her body was a reminder of the child he hadn't chosen to father? When Matt had kissed her for the first time after their agreement to start seeing each other again, her belly had touched his and Matt had moved away as though he had been burnt. Physical contact since had been almost platonic. Until last night, that was.

'Seven o'clock, then? Not too late?'

'Ah…no. Seven's fine.' Polly had to consciously recall what Matt had been saying. He was arranging a date. A meal at the restaurant by the beach in Sumner. The first romantic date that had been arranged in the last month. And Polly knew without a doubt that Matt would take her home to his apartment afterwards. The promise that had been expressed in last night's kiss was going to be honoured. Polly took a deep breath.

'Must go,' she said hurriedly. 'I've got some drugs to collect. I'll see you later, Matt.'

Polly tried to remember what it was she was going to collect but failed. All she could think about was that kiss. Matt had taken her home after an evening spent with the Weavers and he had kissed her in the car. For the first time since he had learned about the baby, Polly had felt a connection that had reminded her of what they had once had. It had only been there for an instant but it had been enough to give Polly a glimmer of hope and to remind her of what she really wanted from the man she would be prepared to marry. It could easily have been enough for that kiss to lead on to much more but Matt had pulled away and Polly had not been confident enough to ask him inside. Tonight would be a different story. Matt wanted more as well. She had seen that in his eyes when he had checked that the time arranged for their date was suitable. Polly drew in a deep breath, wondering whether it was anxiety or excitement that had prompted the need for some extra oxygen.

She pulled a scrap of paper from her pocket. Bicarbonate and potassium. She was muttering the required doses to herself as she entered the drugs room to find Stephanie squeezing Ventolin into a nebuliser mask.

'How's Melanie?' Stephanie queried.

'Coming right, I think. Her blood-glucose level is falling and her blood pressure's up a bit so she's not so dehydrated.'

'That's good. If you get a free minute I could do with a hand in Room Three.'

'Busy?'

'Flat out. I've got two cases of bronchiolitis, one of exacerbated asthma and there's a baby with croup on the way up from Emergency. And there's an outbreak of RSV going around.'

Polly nodded as she scanned the shelves for the drugs she needed. Respiratory syncytial virus usually led to an influx of young children with breathing problems. Polly selected some syringes to draw up Melanie's medications.

'How did the date with Matt go last night?'

'Great. We had dinner with Karen and Russell again. Sophie is the most gorgeous baby.'

'Not a romantic evening for two, then?'

'No.' Polly found herself smiling as she expelled

the air from the syringe. 'But he's taking me to a restaurant by the beach tonight. One that we had rather a romantic evening at a while ago.'

'Aha!' Stephanie gave Polly a meaningful glance. 'He's about due to propose again, isn't he?'

'Mmm.'

'I hope you're planning to say yes.'

'I don't know. Probably not.'

'You'd be mad not to.'

'Maybe. But I'm not going to marry just because everyone expects me to. Or because it will mean financial security. I need to know that Matt wants *me*—not just a housekeeper or a nanny for his child.' Polly hesitated. 'Or that he just wants the baby and not me at all.'

'How will you know?'

Polly sighed. 'I don't know. Maybe I won't know until after this baby is born.' Even tonight was going to have the extra dimension the baby provided. What would love-making be like with their baby sharing the contact of their bodies? How would Matt feel when he could place his hands on her bare skin and feel the movement of his child? Perhaps any chance of knowing whether Matt wanted her purely for her own sake was already long gone. And perhaps Polly still wanted Matt badly enough to accept whatever he was offering. Except for marriage. By holding on to her principle of not making that commitment to someone who didn't feel the same way she did, Polly could almost convince herself that she would be retaining both her integrity and a level of self-protection.

Matt held the button on his Dictaphone down.

'The initial incision was extended upwards and laterally to gain access to a retrocaecal appendix. Haemorrhage was controlled in the usual manner.'

Matt paused. His mind was not really on the task of catching up with his paperwork. Having finished his ward round shortly after arranging his date with Polly, he now found it rather difficult to concentrate. Control was the key to many things other than haemorrhage during routine surgery. Matt had control in his personal life as well. And he intended to keep it.

It was simply a case of shifting fences. He knew how close he had come to falling head over heels in love with Polly Martin but that kind of loss of control could easily be contained. He knew the kind of love it was possible to have for one's child but that, too, could be contained. The fences didn't need construction. They were there already, formed by scar tissue and unlikely to ever be toppled. Matt knew he wasn't capable of offering either of those kinds of love again. The scars were quite thick enough to offer any protection he needed against being sucked into the selfless, potentially soul-destroying relationships that marriages were ideally based on.

That didn't mean that his marriage to Polly would need to be less than ideal, however, for either of them. The fences could be moved a little. He would love, honour and respect Polly. He would provide and care for her and for any children they had together. He could even feel excited at the prospect of sharing his life on a permanent basis. To have a family to come home to. To watch their children grow up. To wake up next to Polly every morning. Matt hadn't forgotten the sense of deep contentment he'd felt the morning after his bone-marrow harvest when he'd woken to find himself in Polly's arms. Contentment was fine. Better than fine. He would welcome it.

Neither had Matt forgotten the other emotions that came from Polly sharing his bed. He could welcome desire as well. In fact, he had been welcoming it in increasing quantities for the last four weeks—ever since Sophie Weaver had been born. He had put off taking Polly to bed again, though, partly due to a nervousness about making love to a pregnant woman and partly because he hadn't wanted her to think that sex was a major incentive in the reestablishment of their relationship. Matt still regretted that remark he'd made. The steps he'd taken to bring them closer over the last month had been carefully taken. Matt had a clear goal here and he was in control.

Polly would accept his next proposal because he was going to offer everything she needed. And he was going to be safe because he knew he had control. Being with Polly and even having a baby were things he could cope with because they were going to be bonuses. He had survived without Polly while he had been overseas and he could survive without her again if he had to. She was a bonus. Not a vital component of his future happiness. The baby would also be a bonus, and now that Matt was clear about his limits he was happy to take things further.

Tonight he would take Polly back to his apartment. Reinstating their physical relationship had been coming steadily nearer and the kiss they had shared only last night had left Matt in no doubt what Polly's response would be. Lord, he'd almost lost control then—the instant he'd felt her response. It had been the final test he'd needed. He had been able to draw back, to walk away even, knowing that he could give and receive any level of physical communication without any real threat to his protective barriers. Maybe the fence was, in fact, a wall and there was nothing behind it any more to feel afraid of. Maybe that abyss had been filled in. Covered over and obliterated just as Bonnie's grave had been. The site was marked, not with a headstone but with a wall. A wall of safety.

Matt felt renewed confidence as he brought his Dictaphone nearer his mouth and prepared to get back to work. Tonight was the night he would propose to Polly again, and what better time than when they were in each other's arms, having made love? She couldn't possible refuse this time.

'No. I'm not going to marry you, Matt.'

Matt was stunned. His control of this situation had just been taken away. Instinctively, his hold on Polly tightened a little. He was getting used to this peculiar sensation of her hard, rounded abdomen pressing against him. He liked it. If anything, the change in their love-making that Polly's shape had dictated had made it more exciting. The passionate encounter they had just shared had been more fulfilling than any sex Matt had ever had. Polly seemed to have reciprocated his feelings. So why the hell had she just refused his proposal again?

'I don't understand,' Matt said slowly. 'We enjoy each other's company, don't we?'

'Yes.'

'The sex is amazing. At least, I thought it was.'

'Oh, it was amazing all right.' Polly shifted in his arms and planted a soft kiss on the dip beneath his collar-bone.

'We both want the best for our child, don't we?' Matt's hand strayed back to Polly's abdomen. He was still getting used to the feeling of their baby moving inside her, unpredictable little wriggles and kicks that had made his first very close encounter with a pregnant woman an unforgettable experience.

'Of course we do,' Polly agreed quietly. She loved the feeling of Matt's hand on her belly, connecting her baby to both its parents.

'And I...love you. You said you love me, so why won't you marry me?'

Polly propped herself up on one elbow. 'It's because I love you that I can't marry you.'

'That's crazy.'

'No,' Polly gave her head a tiny shake. 'I *really* love you, Matt. The kind of love that means I could never walk away. Never give up. Never stop loving you. You don't love me like that. You *did* walk away.'

'Because I had to. Because I was afraid of how strong my feelings were.'

Polly nodded. 'I know. And ''were'' is the right tense. We had magic between us once, Matt. That night on the beach when you kissed me and I told you that I loved you, I could feel it. You didn't say you loved me but I *felt* it. I've never felt that way before and if I hadn't met you I wouldn't have known that love like that even existed. Do you understand what I'm talking about?'

Matt was silent. Of course he understood. He had felt it, too. A space he'd never been in before. A shared love that had been far greater than the sum of its components. A space he could have entered and remained inside if he hadn't learned how great the pain of being expelled could be. Now that space was well behind the wall in his heart. Even further back than the space Bonnie had claimed.

'Magic doesn't exist,' he said, more harshly than he had intended. 'Or, if it does, it doesn't last.'

'Sometimes it does,' Polly said quietly. 'Look at Karen and Russell. The way they look at each other and touch each other sometimes. They still have it after all their years together and all the pain they've gone through. If it's not there to start with then there's no chance of having it later. I don't want a marriage without that magic. It's what my mother settled for. Probably what a lot of people settle for, but it's not enough for me. Not now that I know what it can feel like.'

'There you go,' Matt said. 'You said you only felt it because you met me. You might not find it with anyone else.'

'I'm sure that's true,' Polly responded. 'The problem is that *we* don't have it any more, Matt. It's gone.'

'Maybe it will come back.' Matt tried to sound optimistic. It was difficult because he knew quite well how inaccessible that space was now.

'Maybe it will.' Polly's sigh suggested that she recognised the barrier. 'When it does—*if* it does—then I'll know because I'll be able to feel it. That's when I'll marry you, Matt. Not before.'

Matt needed to move. He swung his legs off the bed and rose. Knotting the cord on his dressing-gown, he finally turned back to Polly who was now sitting with the sheet pulled up around her.

'What if it doesn't come back?' he asked. 'Does that mean you'd walk out on me?'

'I don't know.' Polly's eyes were huge in her pale face. Matt had the impression that she was finding this conversation as difficult as he was.

'Love has to be based on trust, Polly. How can I be expected to love you as completely as you want if I can't trust you not to walk out on me?'

'The same way I'll have to trust you not to walk out on me. And you've already done that once.'

'And you broke my trust by not telling me you were pregnant.'

'I told you why.'

'And I accept that. Your reasons were as compelling as the reasons I had to get away for a while. We both have things to forgive, Polly. Maybe we need the commitment that marriage would represent in order to trust each other enough again.'

'Marriage isn't some kind of insurance policy.'

'But you're not even prepared to make the kind of commitment that indicates our relationship has any chance of long-term success. You're not being fair.'

'I'm not being any more unfair than you're being. You can't give me the kind of commitment *I* need.'

'But—'

'I'm talking about emotional commitment, Matt.'

Matt sat on the end of the bed with a sigh. He couldn't understand any of this. He was offering everything he could. 'But I love you. I mean that. It's not something that's even easy for me to *say*.'

'I know that, Matt,' Polly said gently. The sincerity in Matt's words was obvious. 'I hear you say it but I don't *feel* it. It's not enough. Not yet.'

'I want to be with you.'

'I want to be with you, too.' Polly couldn't imagine wanting to be anywhere else.

'I want my child to have my name.'

'He will.'

'I want to be there to see him growing up. I want to live in the same house as my son—the same house as you, Polly.'

Polly was very close to tears. Was it his son he really wanted…or her? And did it really matter? Being with him like this and knowing that he wanted her at all was enough to offer sustenance to a starving soul. Against all her better judgement and resolution she was almost prepared to take the risk and accept what Matt was offering. To live with the hope that it would be different from her mother's fate. Matt had loved her. He might heal enough to do so again. If she was patient enough. She had far too much to lose not to allow the opportunity.

'Let's compromise, Matt,' Polly suggested. 'We'll live together. We'll share our lives and our baby. Maybe that's the only way we'll ever know if it's going to work.'

'But you won't marry me.'

'I can't. Not yet, anyway.'

Matt was silent for a long minute. Then he stood up again, walked to Polly's end of the bed and leaned towards her.

'I'm not going to propose to you again, Polly.' A small smile indicated that Matt had accepted the compromise Polly had offered. 'We'll find a house and live together and I'll give you everything I would give you if we were married. But if—I hope, *when*—you change your mind, it's you who'll have to do the proposing.'

Polly's heart ached for the sincerity she could see in Matt's eyes. The pain of knowing he was no longer capable of giving what she was asking for. Yet he still wanted to give her what he could and Polly loved him even more for that. She reached up to touch his face and then pull him closer so that she could kiss him.

'It's a deal,' she whispered.

CHAPTER NINE

IT WAS a new beginning.

The month following Polly's second refusal of Matt's proposal was wonderful. Polly moved into Matt's apartment and began seriously looking for a house. They saw as much of each other as their shift work allowed. Shared shopping and cooking duties, meals, conversations and quiet times. Shared nights that drew them closer again. As close as they had been right at the beginning—when Polly had known how attracted she had become to Matt but before she had recognised how deeply in love she was and how much she wanted her feelings reciprocated.

Keeping those feelings at bay seemed possible, however, and Polly was grateful for what they had. She could, almost, take Matt's point of view and persuade herself that it was enough to base a marriage on. Especially since Matt was clearly making an effort himself to move in the other direction and show Polly that he was capable of more, rather than less, emotional depth. And it was working. All it needed was a genuine flash of the magic Polly knew was possible and she would have no hesitation in keeping her end of the deal and proposing.

She almost did it the day they found the house.

In a month of viewings Polly had not been able to find anything that Matt was remotely interested in. And no wonder! When Matt contacted the real estate agent he promptly tripled the price range she had confined herself to. Within a week they had been shown a property on the hillside above Sumner beach. Polly was silent throughout the first tour until the agent had left them alone to consider any offer they might like to make.

'What do you think, Polly?' Matt looked as excited as he had the day they had taken Bonnie to Tiger Island and Polly's love for him was so strong it felt like pain. She had to bite back a sudden impulse to choose an inappropriate place and time to propose. She simply smiled instead.

'It's perfect,' she said.

'It is, isn't it?' Matt waved a hand towards the panoramic view of the surrounding hills, the sea and the foreshore, which included a familiar restaurant and walkway. 'This place has everything. Warmth, space...a fabulous view. Imagine sitting on this deck and watching the moon come up over the sea.'

Polly could imagine it just as clearly as she could remember the time they had admired the moon's reflection on the ocean from ground level. Maybe this wasn't such an inappropriate place to propose after all. If Matt stopped talking for a moment, she might do just that.

'There's a four-car garaging with drive-on access. That's not easy to find on the hill. The swimming pool's fenced so it's safe and there's even a children's play area.' Matt frowned as though concerned at how quiet Polly was being. 'The garden's not too big, is it?'

'The garden is amazing.' Polly looked down the wide steps towards where the hillside had been cleverly terraced into a series of garden rooms. Below the deck was an intimate courtyard with an outdoor open fire and barbecue facilities. Below that was a summer garden with a gazebo, a rock pool and dozens of rose bushes. Around the corner was a fenced terrace housing the swimming pool and outdoor spa and the level below that boasted a playhouse, sandpit, swing and slide. The lowest terrace, bordering the property, had been turned into a woodland area with enticing paths to explore and secret places for children to create their own world. Together with the modern and very tasteful living spaces the house provided, it was the kind of family home Polly had only expected to dream about.

'It's all perfect, Matt. I love it.'

'It has the right feeling, doesn't it?' Matt nodded with satisfaction. 'I knew it as soon as we walked in. None of the other houses we looked at had it. Not even a hint of it.'

'No.' Polly bit her lip and the inclination to propose to Matt faded suddenly. How could Matt recognise magic in a house and be so sure that it was what made the difference when he couldn't see how important that same kind of magic was in a relationship? This wasn't the time to discuss it, however. Not when Matt looked happier than she had seen him in so long.

'Let's see how soon we can move in,' Matt decided. 'We only want a week or two to find all the extra furniture we'll need.'

It was another four weeks before the settlement date on the property transaction. Four busy weeks that left Polly feeling every day of her advanced pregnancy. She was tired and it seemed to take too many days to try and arrange their new house the way they wanted it. Matt was slow to connect up the spaghetti of computer cables in his office and crates of books lay in the living areas waiting for the custom-made bookshelves that were well beyond their promised delivery date.

'You should stop work,' Matt advised. 'You need to rest and get ready for this baby. We haven't even started getting the nursery done yet.'

'I've cut my duties back. I'm only going to work three shifts a week from now on and I've only got three weeks of work to go, anyway. They're so short-staffed,' Polly told Matt. 'I'd feel awful if I just walked out now.'

'Waddled out, more likely.' Matt grinned.

'Thanks, mate.' But Polly had smiled. She welcomed the teasing, just as she welcomed any sign that Matt's sense of humour was returning to the days when Bonnie had been alive. Surely it was only a matter of time until Matt healed enough to be able to really love her again.

By the following week Polly was fervently wishing she had taken Matt's advice and taken her maternity leave earlier than planned. If she had, she wouldn't have been involved in the case of Jamie Broadbent and she wouldn't have realised just how far away from healing Matt still was.

It was bad luck they were so short-staffed. Polly had agreed to take on the duty of seeing a new arrival settled into Room One—Bonnie's old room. The orderlies must have been short-staffed as well and it took so long for Jamie to arrive on the ward that Polly's shift was due to finish, but there were no other staff free so Polly felt obliged to stay. It shouldn't take too long to settle in Jamie and his mum, and Matt was often late to collect her after a shift anyway.

Polly's confidence in getting off duty quickly faded as soon as she saw her patient.

This baby was sick. Six-month-old Jamie Broadbent looked a lot worse than the call from the emergency department had suggested. Polly had seen many cases of croup both here and in Emergency, and while Jamie had signs of respiratory distress with a rapid rate of breathing, tracheal tugging and retraction of the muscles around the rib cage, he was not producing the expected noises of stridor on inhalation or the distinctive barking 'seal' cough. Polly noticed that the infant was mouth breathing and producing a short croaking sound with each inspiration.

'How long has he been drooling like that?'

Jamie's mother wiped his face with a tissue. 'He's teething,' she told Polly. 'He dribbles a lot.' She wiped his mouth again. 'Not usually this much, though.'

'He feels very hot.' Polly reached for the tympanic thermometer. 'I'll check his temperature again.'

'They said it was only up a bit. Thirty-eight point one or so. He's been a bit sniffly for days now.' Susan Broadbent sighed. 'I assume it's the same virus his brother had weeks ago. Mark's still keeping us all awake coughing all night.'

'His temperature's up a lot now.' Polly recorded the fever of 40 degrees centigrade as her anxiety mounted. 'Let's get his vest off.'

'At least he's stopped crying.' Susan sat Jamie on her knee and peeled off the woollen vest. 'I think that nebuliser they gave him downstairs must have helped.'

'How long ago was that?'

'At least an hour ago. They were so busy down

there and then we had to wait ages for someone to bring us up to the ward.'

Polly was observing Jamie closely. He wasn't crying. In fact, he was unusually silent for a sick baby, which was often a sign of a serious condition. The baby leaned forward on his mother's knee and a long stream of saliva dripped from his mouth. Alarm bells went off for Polly. The child might have been coughing and have appeared to have a case of croup on admission to Emergency, but he now looked far more like a case of epiglottitis which could be life-threatening.

Susan was wiping away the dribble again. Jamie's mouth was wide open.

'Don't put your fingers in his mouth,' Polly warned.

Her warning came a split second too late. Susan snatched her hand away as Jamie made a hiccuping noise. She threw a frightened glance at Polly and then tipped her baby back to look at him.

'My God! He's not breathing!'

Polly picked the baby up from her arms and laid him on the bed, reaching for the emergency kit on the wall. 'Push that red button over there,' she directed.

Susan leaned on the arrest alarm, staring at Polly with horror. 'What's happening?' she cried.

'He's stopped breathing.' Polly fitted the tiny mask over Jamie's mouth and nose and carefully squeezed the bag attached to the mask. 'He has a swelling in part of his throat and I think it's gone into spasm and blocked his airway.'

Stephanie came into the room at a run, closely followed by Lee.

'Respiratory arrest,' Polly informed them tersely. 'Steph, can you hook this up to the oxygen, please? Run it at fifteen litres.'

'I'll get the crash cart.' Lee turned swiftly. 'And I'll see if there's a doctor anywhere on this floor.'

Stephanie plugged the tubing from the bag mask to the wall oxygen outlet and turned the flow up to maximum. She took hold of Jamie's arm to feel for a brachial pulse. 'Heart rate's slow,' she reported. 'And the pulse is faint.'

Lee came back, pushing a stainless-steel trolley. 'The crash team's on its way,' she said, 'and Kirsty's checking Ward Three to see if she can find someone closer.'

Polly wondered how far away Matt was. He would have been expecting her to have finished her shift by now.

Lee was watching Polly's careful ventilations. 'I'm not getting much air in,' Polly told the charge nurse. 'His airway feels completely blocked.'

'I can't feel a pulse any more.' Stephanie sounded nervous.

'Start chest compressions,' a male voice said calmly.

Lee followed Matt's instruction, placing her fingers on Jamie's sternum, compressing his small chest with rapid movements.

'Was there any trigger for this?' Matt queried.

'Jamie was drooling,' Polly told him. 'He was very quiet and had a fever of forty degrees centigrade.' She was pressing the mask gently to the tiny face. 'It looked like epiglottitis rather than the croup we were expecting, and I think he went into laryngospasm after having his mouth wiped.'

'Oh, my God,' Jamie's mother groaned. 'You mean this is my fault?'

'Of course not,' Polly told Susan. She wanted to reassure her but the situation was too urgent to allow distraction and Polly had the terrible feeling that reassurance might well be inappropriate. She squeezed the bag again gently, desperately trying to coax some air past the obstruction and into the baby's lungs.

'We'll try intubating him. If that doesn't work, he'll need a needle cricothyroidotomy.' Matt pulled a pair of gloves from the box on the wall. 'Someone call for some anaesthetic back-up.'

Stephanie left the room hurriedly as Polly positioned Jamie's head for Matt to insert the blade of the laryngoscope. He shook his head only seconds later as he removed the instrument from the baby's mouth.

'No chance of tubing him. Bag him again, Polly.'

The crash team arrived and suddenly the small room was crowded. Apparatus was found for the drastic procedure of inserting a needle into Jamie's throat to create access to the airway below the blocked portion. It was Matt who handled the modified large-bore cannula and the anaesthetic connections. No longer needed as other doctors took over Polly's role in managing the oxygen supply, she moved to stand with Jamie's mother at the far side of the room. She put her arm around the woman, knowing full well the horror Susan was experiencing but also knowing that it was better for her to see that everything possible was being done to try and save her baby if the worst happened.

The worst did happen. The airway management was successful but the arrest team was unable to get Jamie's heart to start beating again. They worked for nearly an hour before finally admitting defeat. It was only as the IV lines and airway equipment were being removed that Polly noticed the absence of one of the staff members.

'Where's Matt?' she asked the registrar, who was fitting the defibrillator paddles back into the life pack.

'Mr Saunders?' The young doctor frowned. 'I think he left quite a while ago. About the time we got the venous access for drugs.'

He must have left during the bustle of starting the full cardiac resuscitation after the airway had been secured. Nearly an hour ago. Polly stood very still, her gaze drawn to the distressing sight of Lee getting Jamie ready for his parents to hold for the last time. Susan had been taken to the relatives' room by Stephanie to await the arrival of her urgently summoned husband. Polly simply stood and stared, overcome by how dreadful this situation was. A baby was dead and there was nothing at all that anyone could do. She was unaware of the registrar's pointed gaze at her abdomen or the look that passed between him and Lee. The next thing Polly was aware of was the firm arm of the charge nurse around her shoulders. She was being led into the privacy of Lee's office and it was there that she broke down completely and sobbed uncontrollably.

'Where's Matt?' she choked out finally. 'Where did he go?'

'I don't know, love.' Lee handed her some fresh tissues. 'I'll try paging him in a minute.'

'Why did he go?' Polly blew her nose and then held the tissues pressed against her eyes as fresh tears erupted.

'He'd done what he could, I guess,' Lee suggested

quietly. 'Maybe he didn't want to find out that it had been unsuccessful. It's a very distressing situation. Especially for you.' Lee's criticism of Matt deserting Polly remained unspoken. 'I'm sorry, Polly. I wasn't thinking. I should have sent you away.'

Polly blew her nose again. She knew why Matt had gone. He had run away from the emotional involvement the situation had demanded. She swallowed the painful lump in her throat. Polly knew she was going to have to cope with this. On her own.

'It's time I stopped working,' she told Lee. 'I don't think I can handle any more of this job right now.'

Lee nodded but took hold of Polly's hand. 'Not just yet,' she urged. 'Something good will happen and you'll be able to leave and not dwell on the sad memories or start worrying too much about your own baby. Just give it a few more days.' She squeezed Polly's hand. 'I'm going to find Matt for you now and he can take you home. It's him you need a cuddle from. Not me.'

Polly did get a sympathetic cuddle from Matt but it was too little, too late. The case of Jamie Broadbent was not discussed in any detail and Matt dismissed his own involvement in 'just another case'. He insisted that he was not devastated.

'I can't afford to get that involved with my patients,' he told Polly calmly. 'I couldn't do my job if I did.'

Matt knew he had done his best for Jamie Broadbent. He also knew that the reason he didn't share Polly's distress was because he had timed his exit from Room One perfectly—at precisely the same time that personal involvement had threatened to kick in. With the feeling of empathy that had come from the sight of Susan Broadbent's face when he had stepped back from the bed and had noticed that the baby's mother was still in the room. An empathy that had carried the danger of having to relive the pain of Bonnie's last breath.

It had been a timely warning not to rely on things even when they had the seductive appeal of permanence. Things like finding the right house and living with Polly. A source of happiness that could be depended on and which invited increasing emotional involvement. Jamie's case was a reminder that lives could be shattered in the blink of an eye and Matt took the opportunity to stand back and monitor his own situation. Did he really need to rush home after work every day to be with Polly? Did he need to spend every free evening enjoying the pleasure of her company? It was a bonus after all. He should be able to manage without it sometimes.

Matt couldn't afford to get that involved with anyone, Polly decided. The bitter thought surfaced too often in the days following Jamie's death. Matt was spending noticeably less time with her. He often stayed late at work these days and when they were home together there seemed to be an increasing numbers of hours that needed to be spent in his office working on his latest research paper.

It would probably be the same tonight, Polly thought sadly. She was at her kitchen bench, preparing a salad to go with the fish poaching in the oven. Her day off had been spent resting and the hours had been long and lonely. She was glad she hadn't given up work earlier than planned. There would have been far too much time to dwell on the fears she had for her future. And Lee's prediction that something positive would happen had been right. Not only had Polly received the loving support from her colleagues that Matt seemed unable or unwilling to give, she also had the joy of renewed acquaintance with the delightful Katy McInroe.

Katy was back for a comprehensive check that her cancer had been cured. Not only did she pass all her medical tests with flying colours, she was now so adept with her artificial leg that she barely limped. Katy followed Polly like a faithful shadow whenever possible and 'helped' with all Polly's duties, charming other children and parents alike. Polly had changed her mind about the disadvantages of the kind of involvement paediatric nursing demanded. The pleasure of sharing another stretch of Katy's life more than made up for the fortunately rare heartbreak of losing a young patient.

Polly had every intention of returning to work as soon as she could after the birth of her baby. She and Karen had already discussed the possibilities and Karen was keen to provide child care so that Polly could maintain her career. She knew Polly well enough by now to understand that Matt was not yet capable of giving the kind of fulfilment her friend was going to need in her life. But whilst the thought of going back to work part time in the future was comforting, the thought of turning up on the ward the next day was not so welcome. Polly tried to stretch her back a little as she shredded lettuce leaves. Despite the day's rest, her backache had not improved. She had probably lifted Katy too often the previous day, but it had been impossible to resist the generously offered cuddles and kisses. She was also having an increase in the number of Braxton-Hicks' contractions that had been noticeable for a week or so now.

The pain was enough to dampen her appetite as well. Matt looked at her barely touched plate with a frown when they were sitting at the table an hour later.

'Are you feeling all right, Polly?'

'I'm fine.' Polly wasn't going to complain about backache. 'I'm just getting a bit tired of being so fat, I guess.'

'Only a few weeks to go,' Matt reminded her. 'Are you nervous?'

'Mmm.' Polly's smile suggested embarrassment. 'It is pretty scary thinking about it.'

'You'll be fine,' Matt said reassuringly. 'You've got a great midwife and an obstetrician who's promised to be there.'

'People shouldn't make promises they might not be able to keep.' Polly felt suddenly irritated with Matt's bland reassurance. 'What if he's in the middle of a Caesarean or out on the golf course or he's gone to a conference in Miami for a few days?'

'Don't create things to worry about, Polly. None of those things are going to happen.'

'How do you know? Have you got a crystal ball or something?' Matt probably didn't deserve to be snarled at but Polly couldn't help herself.

Matt sighed. 'I wish I had.'

Polly echoed his sigh. 'I wish I had a wand to wave. I could get this all over with safely and stop the waiting and worrying.'

'Do you wish it had never come to this?' Matt queried. 'That you hadn't become pregnant?'

Polly met his questioning gaze. If she hadn't become pregnant she wouldn't be here now—in this house. Or with Matt. She wouldn't have the prospect of holding his baby in her arms. 'No, I don't,' she said steadily. 'Do you?'

Matt hesitated for a second. 'I might have chosen to go about this a little differently but I don't wish it hadn't happened. I'm glad it's happened.' His tone was serious. 'I'm not sure I would willingly have chosen to have another child, Polly. You know why. And I thought I had my future all mapped out. Having a family is an unexpected bonus, I guess.'

A bonus. Not essential. He could do without it if he had to. The message was clear enough for Polly to read but she wasn't prepared to leave things like that. Not in the funny mood she was in now. She was even willing to risk driving Matt off by making a reference to Bonnie.

'This child is going to be yours right from the start,' Polly told him. 'From its first breath. That is, if you want to be present for the delivery.'

'I said I would be.'

'You didn't say you *wanted* to be.'

Matt snorted with exasperation. 'I asked you if you wanted me to be there and you said yes. So I'll be there.'

'I only want you to be there if you want to be there.' Polly couldn't blame Matt for feeling exasperated but she felt like that as well. She was getting fed up with the feeling that Matt was an observer. She wanted him involved on a level that really meant something. He was holding back. He always said the right things but the barrier was still there.

'Of course I want to be there. I want to see my son born, watch him take his first breath—hear his first cry.' Matt abandoned his half-eaten dinner and pushed his plate away. 'I want to be there to make sure you're OK and to give all the support I can. I want… Damn it, Polly.' Matt stood up, his chair scraping roughly over the tiles on the kitchen floor. 'I want you to marry me. I want to know that the mother of my son is prepared to make a commitment to a permanent relationship.' Matt turned away and then swung back to face Polly again. He lowered his voice a little. 'I want to be able to say, ''That's my wife giving birth—to my son. Not my ''girlfriend'' or my ''partner''. I want people to know that I'm prepared to make that kind of commitment.' Matt's smile was a little forced but it was still a smile. 'Any time you feel like proposing, Polly, feel free.'

Polly could feel another Braxton-Hicks' contraction tightening across her abdomen. She shifted in her chair to try and ease her backache. 'I'm not going to marry you to save you the embarrassment of finding an alternative label to refer to the mother of your son. It's not a good enough reason.'

'No reason is good enough for you.' Matt's smile had vanished. This time he didn't turn back as he walked away. Polly heard the door of his office shut a few seconds later.

She sat for a few minutes before clearing away the remains of the disastrous meal. She only needed a single reason. She just wanted what she had had once. Matt's love. A touching of souls. Now Matt's soul had the shutters down so firmly that Polly wasn't sure even the birth of his baby would change anything.

The contraction that started as she pushed herself dispiritedly to her feet was much stronger than any of the earlier ones. And hadn't it only been a couple of minutes since the last one? Polly checked her watch. She would time them as she cleared up—just in case this was actually the beginning of her labour.

They were ten minutes apart. By the time Polly noted the third contraction the timing had shrunk to five minutes. And it was painful this time. It had to be labour. Polly eyed the closed door of Matt's office. She felt so shut out. Shut out of his office. Shut out of his heart. The new pain was strong enough to make her cry out. The door of the office opened almost instantly.

'What's wrong? What's happened?'

'It's... I'm...' Polly clung to the back of a chair. 'I think I'm in labour.'

'God!' Matt's face paled noticeably. 'It's too early. It's weeks away.'

'Not any more. I've been having contractions for hours. The last two were five minutes apart.'

'Why didn't you *tell* me?' Matt took hold of Polly's arm and then let go again. 'Stay there. Don't move. I'm going to call an ambulance.'

Polly tried to follow Matt to the phone. Another pain started and was too strong. She bent over the arm of the couch and hung on. She could feel herself sway dizzily. 'I think I'm going to be sick.'

Matt's arms were around her now. 'Sit down... Easy does it. You're OK, Polly. Everything's fine, sweetheart.'

Polly slid down past the front of the couch to sit on the floor. Matt put one of the large couch cushions behind her back. 'The ambulance will be here soon.'

Polly was shivering and her legs shaking uncontrollably. She wrapped her arms around herself and tried to control the waves of nausea. Another contraction began and this time the pain was so intense that it blocked any other thoughts. Polly screwed her eyes tightly shut and tried desperately to remember the breathing techniques she had learned in her antenatal classes. She opened her eyes to find a collection of items on the floor beside her. An empty basin, another basin full of steaming water. Towels and face-cloths and a blanket.

'What are you doing?'

'Making sure we're ready if this baby decides to turn up before the ambulance does.'

'I'm not having this baby here. I'm *not*!' Polly added panic to the mix of pain and nausea.

Matt was holding both her hands now. 'We'll cope if we need to. If this baby is ready it's going to come, and if it's going to come this quickly it's very unlikely there'll be any complications. It might be a very long time since I came anywhere near an obstetric case, but I'm not totally useless. I *am* a doctor.' Matt was holding her wrist. 'You've got a good radial pulse so your blood pressure must still be fine.'

'I don't want you to be a doctor.' Polly pulled her hand free. 'Go away, Matt.'

'I'm not going anywhere. Are you bleeding?'

'How the hell would I know?' Polly was at breaking point. This wasn't how the birth of her baby was supposed to be. It was turning into a disaster—like everything else in her life.

'We need to find out.' Matt sounded very calm now. In control. Polly clung to the reassurance he was offering. 'Let's get these jeans off you.'

Polly managed to help until another contraction began. It felt like the last one had only just finished. She gripped her bare knees and felt her chin drop down to her chest. She heard a strange grunting sound.

'Try and pant, Polly. Don't push just yet.'

Matt whisked her jeans clear of her feet. He laid a towel between her legs then his fingers were on the elastic of her knickers. Polly heard the fabric rip. A snort of something like laughter escaped despite her pain and fear.

'That's the first time any man's ripped my knickers off,' she gasped, and even managed a kind of grin.

Their eyes met. Polly could see a faint reflection of her own fear in Matt's eyes but it vanished as he returned her grin.

'We'll have to make sure it's not the last time, then,' Matt said. 'I have to say, I quite enjoyed that.'

The moment of connection was brief but it was enough. They could do this if they had to. Together.

And it looked as though they would have to. Polly groaned again and any hint of enjoyment left Matt's features. The contraction brought with it a totally uncontrollable urge to push.

'The baby's crowning,' Matt told her. 'I can see his head.'

Polly had her eyes screwed tightly shut again. She panted until the next contraction and then pushed again.

'Don't push, Polly,' Matt commanded. 'Just breathe for a minute.'

Polly opened her eyes to see the back of her baby's head. Matt felt around the neck to check for the cord placement and then he wiped the baby's mouth and nose. Polly could see the baby turning as the next contraction started. A shoulder appeared and then the other shoulder and suddenly it was over. The baby slid clear with a rush into Matt's bare hands and he carefully transferred the slippery burden to Polly's abdomen. The baby started crying. A healthy wail that suggested everything was going to be just fine, from a baby too big to be considered premature despite being born four weeks early.

Their baby had arrived safely.

They had a son.

CHAPTER TEN

'HE'S gorgeous. Absolutely gorgeous.'

Matt disguised his proud smile by lifting the cup of coffee to his lips. Of all the countless photographs he had taken in the last six weeks, this one was his personal favourite. Sam had learned to smile early and hadn't stopped since. This picture caught a beam that had crinkled his dark eyes and made a chubby face topped with an unusually thick thatch of dark hair an advertisement for all the good things in life. The upward tilt at the corner's of Sam's mouth made his smile very reminiscent of Bonnie's. But this baby wasn't Bonnie. This was Matt's son.

'And you delivered him yourself, I hear.' Lee sounded impressed as she gave the consultant surgeon sitting in her office a curious glance tinged with admiration. 'At home? That must have been quite an experience.'

'You could say that.' Matt nodded. Even now, more than a month after Sam's precipitous arrival, he hadn't tried to analyse the feelings he'd experienced. The fear that something would go wrong for Polly or the baby. The weight of responsibility for their safety and the fierce protectiveness had been overwhelming when he'd held his son in those first few seconds of life outside the womb. The emotional pull had been too huge and Matt had been grateful for the timely arrival of the ambulance crew, the bustle of getting Polly and the baby to hospital and the presence of strangers that made it easy to maintain a professional dignity and personal distance.

'How's Polly?' Lee asked, finally handing the small photograph back to Matt.

'A bit tired. Sam's been sniffly for a day or two and she's been up half the night fussing over him. Other than that, she's fine.' Matt opened his wallet to replace the snapshot. The photograph of his son slipped into the slot behind his credit cards, just in front of the well-thumbed, wallet-sized portrait of Polly feeding the tiger cub. Matt closed his wallet quickly. He'd find an excuse to leave in a minute. A few months ago it would have been unthinkable to be sitting like this, having a gossip about his private life with the paediatric ward charge nurse. Polly had changed his life on more than one level and if he stopped to think about it, it was a little disturbing.

'I must get going.' Matt got to his feet as he slipped his wallet into the back pocket of his pinstriped trousers. 'I'm due in Theatre in ten minutes. Thanks for the coffee, Lee.'

'You're welcome. Tell Polly to bring Sam in to visit us. Karen brought Sophie in last week and it made everybody's day.'

'I'll do that.' Matt left the office and walked away with a brisk stride. Sophie had probably picked up the upper respiratory tract virus when she'd been out visiting and then she'd passed it on to Sam. Matt's step slowed as he passed the wall telephone at the end of the corridor but he dismissed the inclination to ring Polly and find out how Sam was. It was just a cold, for heaven's sake. Nothing to worry about. Matt wasn't about to join Polly in turning into a neurotic first-time parent. He couldn't afford the distraction.

It was still all about control and Matt had weathered the emotional storm of becoming a father again without becoming totally unbalanced. He was giving all he could. Polly seemed to prefer to manage the baby care alone and if she missed his company on the evenings he spent in his office she never said anything. It was becoming harder to keep his hands off her at night but Polly had made no moves to initiate love-making. Maybe it was still too soon after the birth. Matt could live without sex if he had to.

This sideways step into family life was an astonishing bonus. It would be easy to become dependent on it because Matt had never realised how lonely he'd been, but he wasn't going to become dependent. No way. At least, not until Polly decided to marry him and remove the escape clause she had built into their relationship. Maybe then…

Matt stripped off his shirt and reached for the scrub suit in the Theatre changing room. It was going to be another busy day and he'd probably end up staying late at the hospital again, but the distraction was welcome. His job was just as important as his personal life and professional skills were much easier to use than emotional ones.

'He's been crying for over an hour now.' Polly was pretty close to tears herself. She held the phone to her ear with her shoulder, using both hands to push the pram back and forth in a rocking motion. 'And he's hot. I think he's running a temperature.'

'It's a very hot day,' Karen said soothingly. 'That nor'wester must be pushing the temperature up to about thirty degrees. Sam's probably just got what

Sophie had last week. She was grizzly and sick for a day or two and then she was fine.'

'Sam's breathing too fast and he's got a cough. I think it's bronchiolitis. Or croup.' Polly was really trying not to panic. She was a nurse, for heaven's sake. Why did a calm, professional approach desert her when it came to her own child? Maybe it was because she couldn't quite ignore the memory of little Jamie Broadbent who had started out with just a case of sniffles.

'Call Matt,' Karen advised. 'See what he thinks.'

'I can't. He's in Theatre all morning and, anyway, he thinks I'm making a fuss about nothing.'

Karen could hear an echo of despair in her friend's words. She wondered, not for the first time, just how involved Matt was allowing himself to be with his son. Or with Polly, for that matter. 'Why don't I come over?' she suggested. 'You sound like you need a rest. Or at least some company.'

'I'm fine.' Polly took a deeper breath. She could cope. She had coped so far, hadn't she? Sam only had a cold. 'You're right, Karen. I just need a rest. I'll try feeding him again. If I get him off to sleep, I'll have a nap myself.'

'I'll come over later,' Karen said. 'When I've got the washing out. If you're worried, take Sam to the doctor.'

Polly scooped Sam from the pram and sat down on an armchair in the family room that adjoined the kitchen. She kissed his small red face and Sam stopped crying to watch her unbutton her shirt. The distinctive tingle as her breasts prepared to release milk made Polly smile. She loved breast-feeding Sam, just as she loved everything else about caring for her precious baby. He was going to be fine. They both were. They had a beautiful home and a father and partner who was prepared to protect and provide for them. Polly needed to be grateful for what she had and not get so stressed about what she didn't have or what hadn't happened yet.

The moments of reflection that often came with feeding Sam were cut short. Polly watched in dismay as Sam pulled away, his face crumpling in misery again. Then he started coughing. The unmistakeable bark of croup appeared with the third cough and Polly's hold on her baby tightened unconsciously.

'It's OK, darling,' she whispered. 'Shh…everything's going to be fine.' Polly was not really aware of the soothing sounds she was making as her gaze swept the room. Where was Sam's car seat? Her mobile phone? Her car keys? Not that Polly had any intention of taking Karen's advice and visiting her local GP. This was serious. As serious as Jamie's illness had been. Polly was taking her baby straight to the emergency department. She hit the speed-dial button of her phone as soon as she pulled out of the garage. She negotiated the hillside road and the phone call with increasing frustration over the next few minutes.

'I don't care if he's in the middle of a bloody heart transplant,' she finally shouted. 'This is an emergency. His *son* is sick. *Very* sick.' She ended the call abruptly and dropped the phone, picking up speed as she entered the laned traffic on the main route into the city. Why had they picked Sumner as a place to live? It was far too far away from the hospital.

Matt was angry.

Polly was also angry.

They sat, grim-faced, each staring ahead through the windscreen of Polly's car. Matt was driving. Sam lay strapped in his car seat in the back. The toys dangling from the handle of the bucket seat had attracted his attention and a crow of delight punctuated the tense silence in the vehicle.

'Sounds sick, doesn't he?'

The sarcasm only added to the unpleasant atmosphere. Polly turned her head to stare through the side window for a change. OK, so Sam hadn't been facing a life-threatening emergency. She had panicked unnecessarily. A dose of paracetamol had been all that had been needed to bring his temperature down, and the friendly reassurance and thorough check-up by Helen and Polly's other ex-colleagues in Emergency had been all she'd needed to put things into perspective. Almost all she'd needed.

'Have you any idea what it was like for me, receiving that message from you?'

'I don't imagine it was all that traumatic.' Polly kept her gaze averted from Matt. 'It's not as if you gave Sam more than a second glance before you walked out.'

'I left a patient halfway through a major operation in the care of a registrar who wasn't experienced enough with the procedure to feel confident. The patient could have died.'

'I thought Sam was seriously ill,' Polly said tightly. 'Jamie Broadbent's mother thought he only had a cold and he was dead a few hours later.'

Matt accelerated decisively as they pulled away from the lights. 'I can just imagine what they thought in Emergency when you presented a child with a mild viral infection and told them you thought it had epiglottitis. They'll be laughing about it for a week.'

'No, they won't,' Polly snapped. 'They understood exactly why I was worried when I reminded them about Jamie. Those people are my friends. They care about me. And Sam. You didn't care,' Polly added bitterly. 'You took one look and ran off.'

'I'm here now, aren't I?' Matt countered wearily. 'I've got cover for the rest of the day so I could take you home. That wasn't exactly easy.'

'I'm surprised you thought it was worth the bother.'

'Cut this out, Polly,' Matt warned. 'I'm doing everything I can. For you *and* Sam. I've asked you to marry me, for heaven's sake. What more do you want?'

Polly shook her head. She was tired. She was hot. The worry about Sam and the relief of reassurance had exhausted her emotional reserves. 'Maybe what I want is something you're not capable of giving me. Or Sam.'

Matt turned into their driveway. 'And what's that?'

'Love,' Polly said sadly.

Matt made an exasperated sound. 'I love you. I love Sam.' He pushed the control to open the garage door. 'I love this house and I love being a family. It's what I want. What I've chosen.'

'You don't see, do you?' Polly said accusingly. 'We're not a family. Not really.' She unclipped her safety belt. 'You go to work—I look after your child and house. I have dinner ready when you come home. You work in your office after dinner if you're not called back to work and I look after your child. You go to sleep. I get up when the baby cries. I feed him. I change his nappies. I comfort him.'

'I do my bit. I've changed a fair few nappies myself.'

'Only when you're asked. You never offer.'

'Why didn't you tell me if it's too much for you? We can get a nanny to help.'

'I don't want a nanny.' Polly's voice rose in frustration at not getting through to Matt. 'I can manage all by myself if I need to. I practically am now.' Polly unclipped Sam's safety belt.

Matt slammed his door. 'You're complaining that you do it all and I don't help enough, and then you say you can manage all by yourself. Damn it, Polly. Make up your mind. What is it that you *do* want?'

Polly reached into the car seat. Sam grinned at her as she picked him up. Polly's tone softened. 'I want my baby to have a father.'

'He's got one.'

'A real father.' Polly met Matt's angry stare without flinching. 'Someone who cares about him so much that he's more important than anything else. Someone who *wants* to hold him. *Wants* to be there to comfort him when he's sad. Someone who feels at least a little bit scared when he gets sick.'

Matt was silent as he followed Polly into the house. The black fear that had threatened to engulf him when he had received the message about Sam this morning had been hard to hold at bay, but he had managed. Just. The effort it had cost was the real reason for his current anger.

'I want a partner, Matt.' Polly was determined to go the whole distance now. 'Not someone who pays the bills while I act as a nanny and housekeeper. That's all I am now, isn't it? You didn't want me. You wanted Sam.' She blinked back tears. 'I don't know why you're bothering to share the same bed. You haven't touched me since Sam was born.'

'You had stitches. You needed time to recover.'

'It's been six *weeks*!'

'You've been too busy with the baby to notice me anyway.' Matt sounded bitter now. 'And when you're not busy, you're tired. Or the baby starts crying.'

Polly ignored the confusion Matt's words were trying to create. The cause always came back to the same problem anyway, one that looked like they were never going to resolve. She couldn't marry this man. Right now she didn't think it was going to be possible to even continue living with him.

'How long do you think you can keep this up, Matt?'

Matt looked wary. 'Keep what up, precisely?'

'Keeping yourself protected. At a safe distance.' Polly sighed heavily. She couldn't put off saying this any longer, even if this conversation was going to spell the end of their time together. 'It's not that you're incapable of loving people—we both know that. It's a case of "won't", not "can't", and that's not good enough. I've given you time. Lord knows, I've been patient. It's been eight months since Bonnie died, Matt.'

Matt looked as though she'd hit him. 'I'm over Bonnie's death,' he said evenly. 'It has nothing to do with this.'

'Oh, come *on,* Matt.' Polly rocked Sam in her arms. He was almost asleep. 'You *loved* Bonnie. Really loved her. She died and that hurt.' Polly's tone gentled. 'I know how much it hurt. But some time... somehow you're going to have to move on. You won't avoid pain by not letting yourself care.

The only thing you'll avoid is the other side of the coin. The joy that comes by taking the risk of really loving someone.' Polly eased the sleeping baby into his pram. 'If you took the time to think or talk about it properly, instead of just locking it all away, you might realise the truth before it's too late.'

'What's that supposed to mean?' Matt's stare was challenging.

'I'm not going to break my heart putting everything I have to give into a relationship that's never going to be good enough.' Polly took a deep breath. 'We'd all be better off if we just called it quits right now.'

Matt took a step towards Polly. 'I'm giving all I can. That *has* to be enough.'

Polly took a step backwards. 'Well, it's not enough.'

'So what are you saying?'

'I don't know.' Polly rubbed her face with her hands. 'I need to think. I need some space.' She looked down at Sam who was sound asleep with his tiny fists curled on either side of his face.

'Sam should sleep for at least an hour so. I'm going to go for a walk. If he happens to wake up earlier than that, there's some expressed breast milk in the fridge.'

Matt let her walk past. They both needed some time to themselves before something was said that made this situation irreversible.

Polly eyed her polar fleece jacket hanging over the back of a kitchen chair. She was hardly likely to need that when it was still hot enough to fry eggs outside. She gave Matt a long glance as she reached the front door but he didn't turn.

Polly opened the heavy door and then shut it quietly behind her.

CHAPTER ELEVEN

THE rumble of thunder advertised a rapidly approaching storm.

'I hope Polly gets back before it starts raining. That southerly is coming through fast.' Karen looked up to stare through the window for a moment before throwing Matt an anxious glance. 'The temperature must have dropped nearly twenty degrees in the last hour.'

'I'm sure she'll be back any minute.' Matt was reassuring himself as much as his visitor. He watched as Karen turned Sophie onto her back again to complete the nappy change. Sophie had just learned to roll over and was practising the new skill as often as possible. Karen leaned over her daughter, placing her mouth on the infant's tummy. She blew a noisy raspberry and Sophie squealed with delight.

Matt laughed and then wondered why the sound seemed odd. When was the last time he had laughed out loud like that? Karen grinned up at him from the floor.

'Isn't she just the most beautiful baby in the whole world?'

'Of course.'

'Mind you, Sam runs a close second.' Karen held Matt's gaze for a long moment. 'And Bonnie was the world's best as far as we were concerned. Love-tinted spectacles, I suppose.' She tickled Sophie. 'Hello, Piglet!'

Matt could almost feel Bonnie's presence in the

room. He leaned forward in his armchair, suddenly serious. 'Do you worry about Sophie, Karen?'

'Of course.'

'I mean more than just worry. Real fear.'

'Of course,' Karen repeated. 'Every parent does. It comes with the territory, Matt.' She smiled. 'I know Polly overreacted with Sam this morning, but I understand perfectly. She loves her baby.'

'I love my baby,' Matt protested.

Karen gave him a very direct look. 'Do you, Matt? Do you love Sam as much as you loved Bonnie?'

Matt swallowed hard. He looked away. 'I can't live with that kind of fear again,' he said quietly.

'Your baby is not going to die, Matt,' Karen said gently.

'You can't know that.'

'No, I can't,' Karen agreed. She looked even more serious than Matt now. 'But what I do know is that you've got to believe that. If you don't—if you hold back loving in case something terrible happens—then you're the one who's going to lose in the long run. If you're not prepared to give all you can, you're not going to receive it either, and that wouldn't be really living in my book.' She gave Matt the kind of warm smile that only a long and deep friendship could produce.

'If we'd held back from loving Bonnie because we knew what was coming then it would be so much worse now. We wouldn't have the treasure of memories that come from the love we gave her and she gave us. And we'd have to live with the knowledge that we hadn't given all we could.' Karen's smile broadened. 'Love's an amazing commodity, Matt. The flow is always there unless we choose to turn the tap off. And the funny thing is that if we do turn the tap off, it's us who wither up and die of thirst.'

A second crack of thunder seemed to come from directly overhead. The room had darkened perceptibly during Karen's short speech and now the pelt of heavy raindrops spattered against the plate-glass windows. The sound was enough to wake Sam from a very solid sleep, and his cry prompted Matt to rise swiftly.

'Wow, are you soggy or what?' he asked his son as he lifted him from the pram. 'We'd better do something about that nappy.'

Karen watched as Matt dealt rather inexpertly with the sticky tabs on the disposable nappy. No raspberry-blowing for Sam. Karen frowned.

'How long has Polly been gone now, Matt?'

Matt checked his watch and swore softly. 'Two hours.'

'And when did she say she'd be back?'

'She said she thought Sam would sleep for an hour and she implied that she'd be back in time to feed him.'

Karen hesitated for just a moment. 'Was everything all right when she left? Between you two, I mean?'

'We'd had a row,' admitted Matt. 'We both needed some space.'

'I had a feeling that might have been the case.' Karen chewed her lip. 'What was she wearing?'

'Just a light shirt. And shorts.' Matt glanced towards the kitchen chairs. 'She didn't even take her polar fleece.'

Sam announced that he needed more than a dry nappy to feel happy by increasing the decibel level of his cries. 'It's all right, mate,' Matt told him.

'There's some milk in the fridge. Maybe Aunty Karen will heat it up for you while I go and see where Mummy's got to.'

'No, you stay and feed Sam,' Karen suggested. 'He's not used to a bottle so he'll take it better from you. I'll go and have a quick look up the road. Watch Sophie for me?'

'Sure.'

Matt heated the breast milk carefully in the microwave and then sat where he could feed Sam and watch Sophie at the same time. The youngest Weaver was happily practising her barrel roll on the play mat. Sam protested vigorously at the unexpected invasion of a fake nipple in his mouth but he was too hungry not to give it the benefit of the doubt after repeated efforts on Matt's part. The familiar taste was enough to allay the baby's suspicions and he latched on and began sucking seriously, the steady gaze from his wide eyes locking with that of his father.

It wasn't just the first time Sam had been fed with a bottle. It was also the first time he had been fed by his father. And it was the first time Matt had experienced this prolonged and rather intimate eye contact. He couldn't look away. Lovers could hold eye contact for a long time but this was different. It was as comfortable as gazing into a mirror. It was like Matt was staring at a part of himself that had somehow broken free. He had never felt this kind of closeness with anyone. Ever.

Sam had him hypnotised. When he stopped sucking and grinned up at Matt with that quirky upward tilt of his lips on either side of the nipple, Matt found himself grinning right back like a reflection. He could feel the connection with this little being right through to his soul. Right through to the place he had thought impenetrable and then beyond it to somewhere completely new. It wasn't that the scars had vanished, they had simply split open, quite painlessly, and Matt had a moment of pure and utter joy as he basked in the love that connection conveyed.

Sophie's gurgle brought his attention back to his surroundings with a jerk. The reminder that Karen was still gone and Polly still missing brought a prickle of fear, and Matt realised that it wasn't just the immeasurable love for his son that had been awakened. Karen had told him exactly what Polly had been trying to tell him for so long. This time he had actually heard the message, and they were both right. He wasn't really living if he couldn't love someone completely. And he was still capable of giving that kind of love. He loved Sam.

And he loved Polly. Their baby was doubly precious because he was also part of the woman that he himself loved. Really loved. Where was Polly? What if something had happened to her and he had never told her how he really felt about her? How could he ever live with that knowledge?

The front door flew open and Matt leaped to his feet. Karen came in, her wet hair plastered around an anxious face. Matt looked past her, seeking Polly but knowing that she wasn't going to be there.

'I couldn't see her, Matt, and it's freezing out there.' Karen's words were distorted by her shivering. 'I think we'd better call the police.'

Only her anger and despair fuelled Polly enough to keep up her determined walk for such a long way up the hill. She left the houses behind and took a track that wound through farmland to the very top of the hills. Despite her exhaustion, her brain refused to slow down. Was there any truth in Matt's suggestion? Had she concentrated on Sam and excluded Matt, feeding her resentment at his lack of involvement by subconsciously pushing him even further away? Or was there more truth in her fear that she was becoming just like her mother and would spend her life living for scraps of real affection and meaningful contact, with her own love finally dying from lack of nurturing? She had overreacted badly this morning, that was true enough. No wonder Matt had been so embarrassed. And angry. And now she had made everything so much worse.

The heat and the strenuous physical exertion finally took its toll and Polly gratefully used the excuse of reaching a landmark to stop walking. She had found this historical site on her first walk along this track when she had had Sam in a front pack. They had taken the walk many times since as part of Polly's post-pregnancy fitness programme. The concrete ruins were the remnants of gun emplacements that had been built but never needed during the Second World War. The walls of the bunkers were covered with lichen and they had crumbled to a small part of their original height, but they were quite enough to provide a good place to sit and rest—to rest and possibly indulge in the release that only a good cry could provide.

Polly buried her face in her arms and gave up trying to find her way out of the emotional maze she was in. She needed help and Matt was the only person she could get that assistance from. They needed to help each other. She couldn't force Matt to take emotional risks he wasn't ready for, but she could make it easier for him. And if she loved him enough then that's what she should be doing. What she *would* do from now on. Of course she loved him enough. Polly intended to return home as soon as she had recovered her strength. To return home and talk to Matt.

She certainly had no intention of falling asleep on the cushion of tussocky grass that grew between the concrete walls. The relief that came from reminding herself of how much she loved Matt and the hope that her new resolution would be a positive influence combined with her exhaustion and the heat, and was enough to overcome her before it even occurred to Polly to lift her head from the cradle her arms had provided.

It was the cold that woke her. Bitter cold that had seeped into her bones as she lay in exhausted slumber. Or maybe it had been the thunder. Polly scrambled unsteadily to her feet. How long had she been asleep? And how could the weather have changed so dramatically? Black clouds were roiling overhead and as she stepped out of the shelter of the bunker walls the southerly wind lashed her with freezing gusts. Already fat drops of icy rain were stinging her bare legs and arms.

Polly stood still. She was a long way from home—at least thirty minutes' fast walking—and she was so cold her teeth were chattering violently. If she stayed where she was and crouched behind the walls, she would have at least a little protection from the storm. She was too cold to think clearly. Wasn't that the first sign of hypothermia?

'We won't call the police just yet.' Matt was pulling on an oilskin coat. He rolled up Polly's polar fleece jacket and snatched up his mobile phone. 'I'm going to drive up to the end of the road. There's a walking track that starts there and Polly's used it before.' Matt headed for the door. 'If you don't hear from me within twenty minutes, call out a search party.'

'OK.' Karen was still shivering despite the blanket around her shoulders. 'Don't worry about Sam, Matt. I'll look after him.'

'I know you will. Thanks, Karen.'

'Just find Polly.' Karen bit her lip. 'And make sure she's all right.'

'I will,' Matt said grimly. 'I have to.'

It was less than a minute's drive to where the road ended. Matt strode through the rain on the walkway. He tried not to imagine Polly lying injured somewhere on the track ahead. Or think about what it would be like when a police search-and-rescue operation was launched and he was forced to sit and wait for possibly dreadful news. He would find Polly himself. He *had* to.

He could have walked right past her. The concrete ruins were slightly off the track. If it hadn't been time for Matt to ring Karen and call for assistance with his search, he would have kept going. As it was, Matt knew that the limited shelter would help reception for his phone call. He stepped through the tussocks, his fingers slipping a little on the wet keypad of his phone and he dialled his home number.

'Karen?'

'Matt! Have you found Polly?' Karen's voice crackled and faded. 'Matt? Can you hear me?'

'I can hear you.'

'What's happening?'

'Hang on a second.' Matt lowered the phone as he

dropped to a crouch behind the concrete wall, still stunned by his discovery.

'Thank God,' he whispered. 'Thank God I've found you.'

Polly stared back at him. She could see her own overwhelming relief reflected in the dark eyes locked onto hers. And she could see more than relief. Was her hypothermia so advanced that she was hallucinating? Matt's eyes were so dark they looked black, and it was their intensity that touched her soul. She could see the depth of her own love for Matt coming back to her in equal measure. A connection that was as unmistakeable as the storm raging around them.

Matt reached out and touched her face gently, as though trying to convince himself that she was really there. 'Are you hurt?'

Polly shook her head. She couldn't say anything yet. She couldn't even smile. She was still caught by the intensity of Matt's expression. It wasn't just rain dampening his cheeks. He was shedding tears. The only time she had ever seen Matt cry had been for Bonnie. These tears were for *her*.

'I just realised how much I love you, Polly Martin.' The softness of Matt's words did nothing to hide his pain. 'And I thought it might be too late.'

'It's not too late. I love you, too, Matt.' Polly leaned towards him. There was only one place she wanted to be right now and that was in Matt's arms.

She could hear the high-pitched sounds coming from Matt's phone as he put his arm around her. The sounds turned into words as he raised the phone to his ear just above her head.

'*Matt!* For God's sake... *Tell me!*'

'I've found her, Karen.' Matt's voice cracked despite his calm tone. 'She's all right...everything's all right.'

There was only one cure for hypothermia.

Or so Matt said.

It made no difference that Matt's oilskin coat had protected Polly as he'd carried her along the track. Or that the hot shower had finally stopped her shivering. Or that enough time had passed for Sam to have settled for the night and for Karen to have finally stopped her concerned care and to have gone home to be with Russell. The real cure for hypothermia was body warmth. The kind of body warmth that could only come from the contact of skin against skin.

Polly was only too happy to take the cure. She lay in Matt's arms in their bed and they held each other very closely. The rain had stopped for the moment but the storm had not blown itself out yet. They could hear, very faintly, the sound of waves crashing on the rocky foreshore way below the house. They lay very still. There was no rush to arouse the passion that would come soon enough. For now, the holding was enough. Holding and whispered conversation.

'I love you, Polly. I love you more than I could ever love anybody.'

'I know you do. And I love you, Matt.'

'I really didn't believe I could feel like this again. It scares me, Polly.'

'I know.' Polly held him even more closely. That trust that allowed Matt to take the risk of loving like this again was the most precious gift that Polly could ever imagine being offered. 'It scares me, too. But it's wonderful.'

'It's magic.' Matt returned the increased pressure of Polly's arms. 'I was remembering things when I was walking along that track, looking for you.' He moved his cheek against Polly's hair and she felt a gentle kiss. 'I remembered the first time I really saw you. Sitting in that tree, holding Bonnie. I think that was the moment I fell in love with you.'

'And I fell in love with you the moment I saw you sitting beside her bed. Holding her hand…and crying.'

The kiss they shared then was like nothing Polly had ever experienced. Matt was offering far more than his body. He was confirming his offer of the gift of his trust and love. A love that was as huge as the ocean that still boiled against those rocks below. It was a gift Polly could accept because she could return that love—in equal measure.

'Matt?' Polly's lips were still close enough to touch his as she spoke.

'Mmm?'

'Will you marry me?'

She could feel the smile curling Matt's lips. The smile with that distinctive upward tilt at the corners. The Saunders smile. Matt's smile.

'It's about time you proposed.'

'Is that a "yes"?'

'Mmm.' Matt kissed her again. Very slowly. Very gently. 'That is most definitely a "yes".'